LUNAARA

By Mohit Kamlesh Tolani

Publisher

Power In Me Foundation

ISBN Paperback: 978-93-94749-19-1

ISBN Ebook: 978-93-94749-78-8

Copyright

Publisher

Power In Me Foundation, H.No. 531, MIG-21, Near Subhadra Memorial Hospital, Opp. SBI Colony, Ganiyari Road, Waidhan, District- Singrauli, Madhya Pradesh-486886. Email id: mpowerinme@gmail.com, Mobile: 8851537816

Acknowledgement

Lunaara wouldn't have been possible without the love and support of a few gems. I would like to thank individually.

To begin with I would like to thank Radha Krishn for being my Saarthi in this crazy ride called Lunaara. Every chapter, every turn, every incident, every name felt guided by Something far greater than me.

To my mom Roshni K. Tolani and my dad Kamlesh.S.Tolani. Thank you for being my backbone, even when you didn't fully understand my writings. Your love and discipline shaped both the writer and a human in me.

A special thanks to my chotu, my younger sister Yukti K.Tolani for being my personal editor, My loudest support And my roughest critic all at once. You believed in Lunaara, before anyone else did.

To Manoj Kumar Singh Sir and the entire team at Ruhemohabbat, Thank you for giving Lunaara a platform. Thank you for being my voice. Thank you for believing in me.

To Lady Calypso for being a supportive writer, a good friend and thank you so much for designing such an amazing cover for Lunaara.

About Lunaara

There are stories, and then there are awakenings. Lunaara began not with a plot, but with a series of questions such as
What if the first eclipse wasn't just an event what if it gave birth to a soul. What if paintings cannot just capture images? What if paintings can capture light, Creation and Magic?

This tale was whispered to me not in silence, but in colors. In diamond-faced beings who speak through light. In rogue planets that play music when Walked upon. In creatures who trade innocence for power. I didn't write Lunaara as much as I saw it, As much as I lived through it, as much as I hugged the characters in its world. At its core, this is not just a fantasy. It is a re imagined battle of Light and Darkness but literally. And of a universe that remembers its Beginnings… even when we don't.

I invite you to enter. Where the sky is pink, the trees float upside down, this is Lunaara, and it's not just a story. It is an experience. It's the first eclipse. It's the pulse beneath all things. It's the moment before the universe decided what to become.

TABLE OF CONTENT

Chapter-1: Genesis

In the beginning, there was nothing but **silence**. A silence so profound that it devoured sound itself, and time hesitated to begin its march. In the vast expanse of the universe, amidst swirling clouds of stardust and the birth of newly formed planets such as Earth, one world stood apart from the chaos: a rogue planet named **Kolog**.

Drifting through the infinite void, Kolog had no stars to orbit, no sun to warm its surface, yet it **thrived**, untouched by the rules that governed the rest of the cosmos. The surrounding stars were mere pinpricks of light, casting only the faintest glow on the surface below.

Kolog was a place of **wonder** and **magic**, where the impossible seemed ordinary. The skies were always **pink**, and trees grew upside down, floating in the air, their roots reaching for the sky in defiance of gravity. On Kolog, the silence was broken the moment anything set foot on its lands. With every step, the ground emitted a soft, pleasing tune, as if the land itself played music in response to the touch. The sound was real, clear, and unmistakable—a gentle melody that followed every movement across the soil.

The planet's surface was smooth and untouched, as if sculpted by an ancient hand. Its mountains rose like the crests of ocean waves frozen in time—solid in appearance but liquid upon touch. A trip to these mountains would be like sailing on a river. Despite its otherworldly beauty, Kolog was layered with a blanket of **eerie silence**, as if waiting for something. The mute spectators to this silence were the **Astryns**.

The Astryns were not from Kolog, though they had made it their home since time immemorial. They were beings of pure energy, their forms as transparent as water itself. They drifted through the air like whispers of the wind, silent and eternal. Known throughout the universe as the **silent architects**, they were weavers of reality, the keepers of cosmic balance. Their very presence shaped the fabric of existence.

Kolog was their sanctuary, a place where they could observe the workings of the universe without interference. From this hidden world, they watched the countless births and deaths of stars, the rise and fall of galaxies, and the slow, first march of time itself. Yet, even the Astryns, in all their timeless wisdom, sensed a coming change. There was a stirring in the cosmos, a shift in the delicate balance they had carefully maintained. Kolog, the rogue planet, floating and swinging gracefully, had now come into contact with a space between the sun and the moon. And then it happened: a moment of pure magic unfolded. The moon, a beacon of unblemished light, drifted into the embrace of a shadow cast by Kolog.

"It was the very first Lunar eclipse of the universe."

The celestial event was a divine ballet where light and darkness entwined in a cosmic waltz. As the moon's radiant glow dimmed, it unveiled a spectacle of raw, primordial power. This was when the planet's core pulsed with an ancient, untouched, untamed magic. It was a gray liquid, beating like a heartbeat—slow and steady at first, but growing louder with each passing moment. The Astryns, though silent, could feel the vibrations reverberating through the very air they drifted through. Something was coming. Kolog's pink skies began to change colors, from black to gray to silver. A single pulse of light erupted from the horizon, bright and blinding, cutting through the darkness like a blade. The light caught the Astryns' attention, making their otherwise translucent, diamond-like bodies shine like the brightest suns. The Astryns chose to be translucent, but their true selves were bodies made of diamonds, with faces resembling triangles—a weird yet true combination that the human mind could not fathom. No wonder there was no trace of life on Earth yet.

So the Astryns turned their glowing faces toward the source of this mysterious light, their movements slow and deliberate, but they made no sound. They did not need to. From the depths of Kolog's core, a massive surge of energy began to rise. The rivers of light that floated above the surface twisted and writhed, drawn toward the center of the planet like metal to a magnet. The ground itself began to tremble with notes of music surrounding the atmosphere. If they were creatures like humans, they would have called this a concert and even paid for it. The inverted trees shimmered and glowed, their roots alight with a brilliance that had never been seen before.

The Astryns hovered in silence, their diamond bodies reflecting the chaos around them. They did not fear what was happening, but they understood the gravity of the moment. This was the birth of something greater than themselves.

At first, it was nothing more than a shadow—a dark, formless silhouette hovering within the radiant glow. But as the light swirled and twisted around it, the shape took form, solidifying into something far more magnificent. Massive wings, shimmering with stardust, unfurled slowly, casting a shadow across the musical land. Its body was split into white and black, much like foxes on Earth. It had medium-length bioluminescent deep midnight blue hair, making it appear as though it was made of light and night combined. Its eyes, two pale, innocent orbs of silver light, glowed with an ancient intelligence. A smile that would melt hearts, making even the cutest human babies fade in comparison.

THIS WAS IT, THIS WAS LUNAARA.

Born from the core of Kolog, **Lunaara** was more than a creature, more than a beast; she was a force of nature, the embodiment of the first Lunar eclipse that had occurred before life began on Earth. Her presence was overwhelming; every inch of her radiated cosmic power. Lunaara was a harbinger of a new era. Her birth signaled a shift in the universe, a change that would ripple through the stars and reshape the course of existence.

As Lunaara stretched her wings, yawning, Kolog began repairing itself. The skies turned pinker than before, the light in the rivers glowed brighter, the floating, inverted trees had now begun to dance, and the air had begun to smell fragrant. The stars seemed to dim as though bowing before Lunaara and acknowledging this celestial event. From the furthest reaches of space to the smallest corners of the cosmos, the birth of Lunaara sent shockwaves through reality itself. Stars flickered and dimmed, planets trembled, asteroids melted, and time itself seemed to hesitate, unsure of how to proceed. The Astryns watched in silence as the otherwise silent veil of the cosmos began to stir—a ripple that disturbed even the deepest reaches of the Astryns' understanding.

The air around the Astryn council buzzed with tension as they gathered on the musical lands of Kolog, each step across the soil releasing soft, melodic sounds. Their forms, made of shimmering diamonds, pulsed with a steady blue light—a sign of deep deliberation. Above them, the pink skies reflected their glow, the soft hum of the earth resonating with their thoughts.

First Astryn (A faint pulse of deep blue light—calm, analytical, trying to understand the source of disturbance. A subtle flicker of pale yellow crossed the blue—curiosity):"Something stirs... do you feel that? A disturbance in the balance."

Second Astryn (A sharp flare of crimson—alarm, concern. The brightness increases and shadows dance on the inverted trees):"Yes, and it grows stronger. We cannot let this force continue. It threatens our creation."

Third Astryn (A series of green pulses—confusion, doubt. Then a flash of white—an urgent question. A soft ripple of colors—gray and black—signaling danger):"If we don't stop it now, our creation, Kolog, will be torn apart..."

All Astryns (A slow, rhythmic flash of gold and silver—agreement. The light dims, signifying a conclusion. All three Astryns suddenly flash red—war. Their translucent forms stiffen, preparing for action):"It is time. We will end this before it's too late. The decision has been made; we must neutralize the threat."

Chapter 2: Attack of the Astryns

In the vast ethereal expanse of Kolog, where pink skies met floating, inverted trees, Lunaara lay in serene slumber. Her colossal form, both majestic and daunting, was draped across a bed of bioluminescent flora that cast a gentle, otherworldly glow. The tranquil harmony of the planet seemed undisturbed, yet the stillness felt like a façade.

Above, the Astryns—translucent beings of diamond and cosmic light—watched with an inscrutable gaze. Their triangular faces, devoid of expressions, were framed by the star-speckled void of space. An Astryn cloaked in shadows hovered silently, its intent far from peaceful. In its hands, a medium-sized asteroid, heavy with ancient cosmic energy.

The Astryn's concentration sharpened as it hurled the asteroid with calculated precision. The massive rock sliced through the stillness of the night sky, leaving a streak of dark brilliance in its wake. The asteroid hurled towards Lunaara, its trajectory unerringly true.

The impact was sudden and shattering. The asteroid struck Lunaara's outstretched arm with a deafening crash, embedding itself partially into her flesh. A scar glowing with an eerie golden light formed where the rock had connected. Golden glitter began to ooze from the wound, cascading like liquid stars onto the ground. Lunaara stirred, a loud, mournful screech escaping her lips.

The Astryn, observing from the darkness, was momentarily perplexed. But this brief hesitation was enough for the other Astryns to recognize an opportunity. They gathered, their shimmering forms coalescing into a formidable presence, their purpose clear.

The moment the attack was perceived as effective, the Astryns surged forward with coordinated, ruthless precision. As Lunaara began to rise, shaking off the effects of the initial blow, the Astryns unleashed rapid blows of asteroids. Lunaara, being the kind-hearted creature she was, just kept dodging until it was too much to take. The asteroid shower seemed to be a never-ending affair, so Lunaara, now using her wings, took flight, caught an asteroid mid-air, dug her claws deep inside it, and ripped it apart like a piece of paper. This made the Astryns take a step back in shock. The Astryns took this to be a call for war, and hence they unleashed their full array of powers.

One Astryn, moving with fluid grace, unleashed "**Event Horizon Orbs**"—tiny black holes that flared outwards, pulling in bits of debris and energy, creating a chaotic vortex. Lunaara's immense size made her a prime target, and the orbs began to encircle her, threatening to ensnare her in their gravitational pull.

Another Astryn, eyes blazing with cold intensity, fired "**Frost Balls**." The bolts streaked through the air, their icy glow contrasting sharply with the golden light of Lunaara's blood. Upon impact, the balls exploded into freezing storms, encasing parts of Lunaara's form in a brittle, frosted layer.

Yet another Astryn invoked "**Entropy Surge**," unleashing a wave of chaotic energy that rippled through the air. The wave collided with Lunaara's shimmering body, causing violent turbulence in her protective shroud. The magic of "Entropy Surge" began to degrade Lunaara's body, causing her to flicker and distort.

Lunaara's eyes, now open and blazing with righteous fury, assessed the threat with a mix of anguish and resolve. Her breath deepened, and a dark, swirling energy began to coalesce around her mouth—"**The Eclipse Breath**." This dark beam of cosmic energy, a pure annihilation force, cut through the black holes and freezing balls, pushing back the Astryns momentarily, forming tiny scars on their glistening bodies. Lunaara then spread her wings, their membranous expanse shimmering through the nebula's light, and invoked "**Astral Wrap**." Tendrils of astral energy surged forth, wrapping around the Astryns in a shimmering embrace. The astral energy began to tighten, restraining their movements and disrupting coordination.

Despite the Astral Wrap's restraining power, the Astryns persisted. They summoned "**Void Nexus**," tearing open a massive rift in space. Through this void, faceless voidspawn emerged, their formless bodies swarming around Lunaara.

This intensified the battle into a tumultuous clash of divine powers. Lunaara's "**Nebula Shroud**" enveloped her in a protective veil of swirling cosmic energy, obscuring her from sight and deflecting the voidspawn's assaults. The nebula's dark tendrils lashed out, causing the voidspawn to recoil in disarray.

Lunaara then launched her "**Plasma Bombs**" at her opponents—spheres of intense plasma energy hurling into the dense swarm. The explosion was magnificent, sending arcs of searing light and heat in all directions. The voidspawn were blasted apart, their forms dissipating into the void.

Yet the Astryns retaliated with their full might. The Event Horizon Orbs converged, creating localized black holes that began to pull in chunks of the plasma-infused environment, causing the very musical ground beneath Lunaara to buckle and crack. At the same time, Entropy Surge was unleashed again, accelerating the decay of her body, weakening her defense. If it wasn't for her Nebula Shroud, she would have been murdered by the Astryns.

Lunaara's frustration grew palpable. With a sudden, decisive movement, she invoked Astral Wrap again, this time with renewed intensity. The astral tendrils lashed out, binding the Astryns and the Voidspawn in an intricate web of energy. The struggle was fierce, with the Astryns fighting against the bindings while the voidspawn continued to struggle relentlessly.

In a final, desperate maneuver, Lunaara summoned a concentrated blast of Eclipse Breath, directing it with pinpoint accuracy at the central nexus of the Astryns. The beam cut through the chaos, obliterating the void nexus and disrupting the summoned voidspawn. The Astryns, now reeling from the powerful attack, were forced to retreat, their forms flickering and fading in the wake of the devastation.

The once-vibrant battlefield was now a scene of scorched earth and smoldering remnants. Lunaara stood amidst the ruins, her massive form wounded but resolute. The golden glitter from her previous injuries continued to flow, mixing with the debris and creating a shimmering, almost ethereal landscape. But surprisingly, her blood—the golden glitter—was mixing into the now devastated lands of Kolog only to cure it. The broken, shattered lands now began to turn musical again. The inverted floating trees that were earlier affected by Event Horizon Orbs, Plasma Bombs, and Eclipse Breath had now started to shine like bright diamonds, looking fresh.

As the Astryns withdrew, their forms dimming and retreating into the depths of space, Lunaara's breath became labored. The damage inflicted upon her was extensive—her shimmering body was fractured, and several scars marred her once-glowing skin. Despite her victorious stance, it was clear that this battle, her first battle, had taken a severe toll on her.

From the void left by the retreating Astryns, a new, ominous rift began to open—a subtle hint of what was yet to come. The void pulsed with dark energy, hinting at deeper cosmic forces at play and suggesting the presence of an even greater threat looming on the horizon.

But Lunaara was too taxed to pay any heed to it. She breathed heavily, her glowing silver eyes flickering with exhaustion. The tendrils of magic that had surged through her body were now waning, leaving her almost fragile—an embodiment of raw power on the edge of collapse. The Astryns had fled, their clear diamond bodies tattooed with multiple scars; the damage had been done. The void around her was vast, stretching endlessly in all directions, but within a distance, something glimmered: a shimmering pool of liquid. It pulsed with a faint luminescence, casting a soft, pale glow that seemed to call to her.

Lunaara's body ached as she walked closer. Each movement sent a sharp jolt through her body. The battle had drained all her strength, and the burning in her throat was relentless. Her body's need to replenish was overwhelming. She finally reached the glowing pool and paused. This was no ordinary liquid—it rippled with hues of rainbow colors. The surface sparkled with fragments of white and yellow light, as though stars themselves had melted into this mysterious elixir. It wasn't water, nor was it of any element she had known. But there was something, something mysterious, something powerful that pushed her toward the liquid. With a trembling movement, she lowered her head and took her first sip. The liquid was cool, colder than the deepest reaches of space, but there was something more to it than just the cold. The liquid was beginning to heal the scars on her forehead.

Chapter 3: Eclipse Veil

When suddenly something unexpected happened. Waves of Liquid shimmer and swirl vibrating in harmonies:

Eclipse Veil: "Who approaches the veil of Eclipse?"

Lunaara: The response flows like a gentle current, luminous pulses of light:

"I seek the essence of life to quench this relentless thirst."

Eclipse Veil: The liquid rippled through melodic resonance swelling:

"Thirst is but a whisper of longing. What do you truly crave?"

Lunaara: Soft waves respond a flickering glow illuminating the depths:

"Power to heal to endure beyond the shadows."

Eclipse Veil: A deeper tone emerges, swirling with vibrant colors:

"Power comes at a price-A fragment of your very soul a very heartbeat of your innocence."

Lunaara: Her innocence flickers, uncertainly igniting bright hues:

What is the price of this gift? What shall I surrender?

Eclipse Veil: The liquid churns undulating with radiant light:

Your smile Lunaara. That brilliance which lights up the cosmos, a treasure beyond measure.

Lunaara: Colors dance in her thoughts each hue resonating with both Joy and Sorrow:

A smile? How can a fleeting expression hold such weight?

Eclipse Veil: The liquid swirls faster, deepening in resonance:

It is the essence of joy, a spark that ignites the stars. Give it to me and eternity shall be yours.

Lunaara: Her heart trembles emotions cascading like waterfall of colors:

But what remains of my innocence once I offer it?

Eclipse Veil: An unwavering response filled with warning but also acceptance.

Innocence fades the moment it's given. Once gone, it cannot be reclaimed.

Lunaara: A frantic plea, slow ripples in the glowing liquid fluctuating between panic and hope.

Then what am I without it? What do I become?

Eclipse Veil: The surface of the glowing liquid is now rippling aggressively.

A force, a force so formidable that even the gods will fear.

Lunaara: The liquid is now quiet, no movement, no ripples, no waves.

....

Eclipse Veil: The glowing liquid begins to form tiny colorless ripples almost transparent.

Will you trade your laughter for the strength?

Lunaara: Doubt mingles with longing colors swirling in conflict:

If I accept what becomes the memory of joy?

Eclipse Veil: The liquid glimmers with wisdom, resonating deeply:

Joy transforms, it does not vanish.

Lunaara: The choice hangs heavy in the Air, shimmering with potential:

To lose is to gain, can I bear the cost?

Eclipse Veil: Waves of soothing sound waves urging her to see:

Power is a journey, not an end you can be both fierce and gentle.

Lunaara: The Call of the veil pulses warmly, the decision echoing in her soul:

I must decide power or purity of my heart?

Eclipse Veil: The Liquid now floats in the air glowing, wrapping her in a cocoon of light:

Choose Lunaara. In this choice you will find the truth of your being.

Lunaara: Her heart quickens the weight of eternity pressing down:

What if I lose my way? What if power consumes the light within me? What if power corrupts me?

Eclipse Veil: The veil shimmers, colors swirling in reassurance:

With each choice, a new path unfolds. You are the weaver of your own destiny.

Eclipse Veil: With each pulse, the invitation grows more compelling the horizon of possibilities expanding:

In your hands lies the strength to forge new joys, to be both guardian and nurturer.

Lunaara: Her thoughts dance in vivid shades of hope and fear:

Can I truly retain the essence of my spirit? Even in power?

Eclipse Veil: The liquid pulses with rhythm, resonating with ancient knowledge:

Every transformation holds the essence of its origin. You will carry your light even as you rise. Step forward and embrace the destiny that waits. In your smile lies the key to unlock boundless potential.

Lunaara: As she contemplates the weight of her decision, the waves intensify. The crescendo of sound envelops her urging her forward into the unknown.

Lunaara thought how would she look without her smile. A smile so heart melting it could defeat the smile of a human baby but what of

Astryn's. The looming threat of their return sent shivers down her spine. If she remained powerless, could she protect her world? Could she protect herself? The haunting memory of the past battled flickered in her mind like shadows reminding her of her vulnerability.

Power could mean salvation whispered a darker part of her. It could shield her from her enemies. She could forge a future where darkness would never threaten light again. Yet in that very power laid the seeds of loss. The thought of exchanging a radiant smile, her infectious innocence for mere strength felt like a betrayal a corruption after all.

She could envision herself ageless and formidable. Yet with every moment of triumph a deeper ache settle within her. Would she become a specter of her former self? A guardian devoid of joy? The veil shimmered, a seductive call echoing in her heart. "What if I lose everything that I am?

The moment hung in the air, thick with anticipation as Lunaara stood before the Eclipse Veil, its surface glimmering like a thousand stars caught in liquid form. Her heart raced, the weight of her decision pressing heavily on her. She could feel the pull of the veil, whispering promises of regenerative abilities which meant an eternity unmarred by fear.

With a deep breath, she closed her eyes surrendering to the turmoil that swirled within. This is it, she thought. The echoes of laughter, the warmth of sunlight, and all the moments that had defined her innocence flashed before her like a tapestry woven with joy and light. But just as vividly, the specter of the Astryn loomed, their formidable presence of a constant reminder of the stakes at hand.

She finally whispered a silent farewell to her past, to the purity of her laughter and the soft glow of her innocence. With one graceful movement, she plunged into the veil. The liquid enveloped her, cool and electric wrapping around her like a shroud of vibrant colors. As she submerged the world above faded replaced by a kaleidoscope of sound waves and luminous patterns that danced around her. The liquid coursed through her merging with her very being, igniting every fiber of her existence.

Emerging from the veil, Lunaara was forever changed-Stronger, ageless yet haunted by the shadow of choice, The light within her flickered now mingling with the deep currents of her new found power. She had embraced the veil, but at what cost? As she stood anew the world around her shimmering with possibilities and yet the ghost of her innocence lingered in the air, a haunting reminder of the path she had chosen.

The glade pulsed with vibrant energy as Lunaara felt an itch of restlessness; she wanted to push her boundaries of her newfound powers, to test the very essence of what it meant to be both strong and yet connected to Ology. With determination in her heart, she stepped into a clearing when there was drizzle from the pink skies. This was Rainbow Falls where each drop of waterfall is not merely water but a prism of liquid light bursting into radiant colors the moment it touches the air. These droplets, shimmering like gemstones create a curtain of ever shifting rainbows, filling the air with soft, harmonious hue-Violet,Indigo,Blue,Green,Yellow,Orange and Red. Each blending seamlessly into the next.

The Rainbow Falls with their cascading streams of liquid light stood as the divine symbol of **Eldarion's** blessing upon Lunaara. The falls were no more spectacle-they were a celestial anointing, a sacred exchange of grace between the heavens and Lunaara. In every arc of color she could feel **Eldarion's** silent presence his will woven into these colorful drops of water. For Lunaara was not just a creature, not just a beast but a creature of the eclipse-She was chosen, touched by the divine hand of Eladrion himself.

Chapter 4: Eldarion.

Eldarion resided in a distant planet called **"Junkin". Junkin** was a planet of brilliance its skies a shimmering cascade of colors and light. Every surface, every stone and every gust of wind seemed infused with magic, pulsating with life. Where Ology was mystical in its subtleties-the inverted trees, musical lands and a delicate balance-Junkin was a powerhouse, a planet where magic roared rather than whispered.

Here the Astryn's were at their peak. Their diamond like forms glistened with more power here than anywhere else, their lights blending effortlessly into the radiant hues of the landscape. The skies above shifted constantly with no singular color dominating for long. It was as if the very air was alive responding to their presence swirling in complex patterns of Gold, Azure and Crimson.

The ground of junkin was equally alive growing under their feet with intense energy. Rivers of light like molten silver flowed across the surface filling the land with a constant soft glow. Everything on Junkin exuded magic in abundance. Floating mountains drifted lazily through the air their peaks reaching towards an endless sky. The trees were crystalline structures that shimmered with untamed glitter.

Despite all this magnificence the Astryn's had once found Junkin to be... too much. The overwhelming surge of magic, the constant shift of light and energy, left them restless after eons of dwelling there. They had long ago grown bored of it. And so they sought something different, something more subtle, which lead them to Kolog-The rogue planet. But now after their defeat at the hands of Lunaara, they returned to Junkin, their diamond bodies flickering with exhaustion. They sought the help of one being who surpassed even their strength-**Eldarion,** the one true god.

At the core of Junkin surrounded by the most intense concentration of light and matter sat **"The Temple of Lumina"**-The resting place of Eladrion. Unlike the eternal spire on Ology, the temple here was built from radiant ever shifting light, its structure barely solid as if existed only in the spaces between the moments. The temple floated in air, a space where reality bent and shifted with the currents of Eldarion's immense power.

Eldarion himself was not confined to any singular form. As the Astryn's approached, his essence pulsed through the temple in waves of light and color. He is the cosmic force that shaped all worlds and his energy flowed through every particle of existence. Unlike the chaotic brilliance of Junkin, Eladarion's presence was steady, like a heartbeat that echoed through space. He radiated power but also control, as all the universe's magic bowed before him. His form, if it could be called a form is a swirling mass of radiant light, galaxies and stars spinning within him. He is more abstract than any of the Astryn's could comprehend a force of creation, preservance and destruction. His presence dominated the temple and its light, the Astryn's felt dwarfed despite their own immense power. Eladrion's light shifted beckoning the Astryn's forward. They had come to seek his wisdom, his guidance. Lunaara the beast was way too powerful even for the Astryn's. Her power had caused ripples of shockwaves throughout the universe. Astryn's believed she had become a threat to the universe, to the very fabrics of creation.

But Eldarion's light pulsed with a different truth. As they stood before him they knew he already understood their purpose. Eldarion was omnipotent his awareness stretching across all realms of existence. He had been waiting, watching and now the time the moment had come for him to reveal the deeper truth of Lunaara's role in the cosmic order.

Communication with Eldarion is not done with words but with light and patterns.

First Astryn: A rapid sequence of sharp crimson pulses interspersed with jagged streaks of silver and black pulses across its shimmering diamond body; the light wavers, and then explodes into erratic bursts of Orange:

Eldarion, the threat grows. Lunaara's strength is uncontrollable, her chaos is unrelenting. She destabilizes the universe with every breath. We fear the worst is yet to come.

Eldarion: Soft waves of deep emerald green ripple outward, slowly spreading a calm, radiant pulse of gold. The light weaves into a spiraling pattern, casting steady arcs of silver.

You misunderstand her nature Satyr's my kids, Lunaara's powers is not the destruction you believe. Her chaos is a necessary force born not to destroy but to evolve.

Second Astryn: Flashes of bright red and streaks of violet dart violently across its shimmering diamond body, colliding into patterns of deep blue and grey. They pulse unevenly before dimming:

Her power is beyond measure, beyond control if she is not stopped what is to prevent her from consuming everything we have worked to protect?

Eldarion: A slow deliberate wave of sapphire blue cascades through the chamber followed by golden arcs and faint streams of white. The patterns shift gracefully into a continuous flow of green.

You have seen her power but not her purpose. She was born for a reason far greater than you realize, she is not the end but the answer.

Third Astryn: Quick intense flickers of Orange and Yellow burst through its shimmering diamond body followed by rapid pulses of dark red. The light begins to stutter and crack, sharp flashes of indigo shooting wildly.

An answer? To what question Eldarion? She destabilizes the universe; her existence is a threat to all what could justify this Chaos?

Eldarion: A wave of warm golden light washes over the Astryns fading into deep violet that glows steadily. Soft tendrils of blue and green intermingle, forming rhythmic loops of light.

Lunaara was not born to bring chaos, but to face a threat. A threat mightier than her own power. Her very existence is the key to defeating **"Drakaara"-The True Destroyer.**

First Astryn: Sharp, Jagged flashes of crimson and silver erupt into the air, spiraling into a violent clash of red and violet. The light pulses frantically, filled with tension.

Drakaara? The ancient enemy long thought defeated? We believe his essence was sealed away for eternity. Is Lunaara meant to face her?

Eldarion: Deep, calming waves of emerald and gold ripple through the space, softly swirling in gentle arcs, and a soft radiant pulse of violet follows, steady and unwavering.

Yes Drakaara stirs again, his darkness grows stronger. Lunaara is not a threat to the cosmos. She is the only force capable of facing Drakaara in combat, both physical and magical.

Second Astryn: Bright flares of silver and turquoise began to travel in its shimmering body its movements quick and agitated. Brief pulses of red and orange intersperse, growing brighter with each flicker.

But Lunaara's power is untamed; she cannot control her own power let alone wield it against such a being. How can we allow her to grow unchecked?

Eldarion: Wide, flowing arcs of warm amber and deep blue spread through the chamber, entwinding with slow, deliberate streaks of white light. The glow expands, radiating calm and authority.

You must not fear her power instead you must guide it. Lunaara must be trained, honed like a weapon forged in the fires of battle. Only through your guidance and training can she become what she is destined to be.

Third Astryn: Rapid bursts of green and blue intertwine, forming sharp, jagged patterns. They dare brightly before fading into soft waves of lavender, tinged with streaks of silver.

Guide her? Train her? But how? Her nature is wild, untamable. How can we shape a force that seems to defy order itself?

Eldarion: A steady pulse of golden light fills with the air, expanding slowly and gracefully. Soft tendrils of violet and green

loop through the space forming of intricate patterns of spirals and arcs.

Lunaara's nature is not disorder. It is potential. She requires both physical and magical training, and it is you-Astryn's who must teach her only through your guidance will she learn to harness the power within her.

First Astryn: Soft pulses of silver and blue weave through the space, calming and measured. Gentle flickers of white interlace, forming a final radiant wave of light.

Then we will heed your wisdom, Eldarion we will train Lunaara, both in combat and magic and prepare for the battle ahead. But we remain wary of her power, and what it may yet become.

Eldarion: Soft radiant arcs of golden light fill the chamber, expanding gently into glowing waves of blue and violet. The patterns slowly fade into calm, harmonious pulses of emerald.

Fear not Lunaara will not walk this path alone. She is an ally not a foe. Guide her well and together you shall face the coming darkness.

And with this the Astryn's step out of the Shimmering temple of Lumina on the planet of Junkin. The air is light filed with winds of hum and life and soft clouds. The three Astryn's move in silence contemplating the weight of their recent fight with Lunaara on Ology and the new task handed to them by Eldarion-To train the very creature they fought.

First Astryn: Its form flickers with cool blues and silvers, betraying his unease.

How do we even approach her now? After the destruction we caused… After we tried to end her?

Second Astryn: A sharp red glow passes through it with waves of bright orange.

It is clear Lunaara is a friend not a foe but how do we convince her of our purpose?

Third Astryn: Soft greens and golds shimmer from it, her light gentle and empathetic.

She must be approached with care. We wounded her yes, but we can also heal her.

First Astryn: A sudden continuous bursts of white and blue shimmer through it with patterns of yellow.

But how? Will she confide in us? She would rather devour us than listen.

When suddenly a soft, gust of wind echoes the corridors of the temple of Lumina and from the skies descends a pure white with black almond shaped eyes, 2 tiny hands attached to its side, legs as good as human legs carrying a bright smile comes a walking cloud weighing about 3 ounces. The cloud a being of wisdom and whimsy hovers above them its presence playful and jolly.

Second Astryn: Its body starts shimmering in rainbow colors creating oceanic waves in its body (In excitement). Moments later its diamond body shimmers with silver color.

Hey Puffins oh my god how are you? Where had you been? All along. I am glad you are here.

Puffins: Twinkling bursts of light followed by ripples extracting light tiny bolts of Thunder.

I am so happy to see you guys back in Junkin after eons but no time for pleasantries. I come with a solution.

Third Astryn: A mix flash of green and blue shimmers through its body in confusion merging to waves of dark red.

Solution? But how can you? Lunaara is a beast and a powerful one at that.

Puffins: Chuckling softly sends out a light sprinkle of shimmering dew mixed with tiny bolts of thunder that fizzle harmlessly in the air.

Lunaara is powerful yes but you forget sometimes the simplest gesture speaks louder than any show of force. You need a gift not a rift.

First Astryn: A soft ripple of pale violet light moves through it.

Lunaara already has too many gifts of power.

Puffins: Swirling with excitement, releasing a gentle hum of melody and tiny playful lightning bolts.

Not a gift of power. Not a weapon. Not a power. Tiny creatures. Creatures that weave light into their honey. The sweet radiant and holds no power except to bring joy and happiness even to most sadistic of the hearts.

All Astryn's now begin to flicker a very bright white lights across their bodies in chorus.

You mean the Glitter bees?

Puffin: Twinkling with joy, tiny cracks of thunder giggling around it.

You guys are not dumb after all haha.

And with this Puffin's disappears. The Astryn's now thank puffin. With renewed hope the Astryn's look at one another ready to embark on their journey, the playful breeze of Puffin's energy lingering in the air as they prepare to make peace with Lunaara.

This was the first time in Eons Astryn's were making a decision purely from their hearts and not from their brains. Puffins had instilled a belief in them that even with this simple gift, perhaps they can begin to build trust. The trust needed to forge alliance. The trust needed to guide her and to heal the rift caused earlier.

After all the fabrics of the universe depended heavily on this new hopeful alliance between Lunaara and the Astryn's. Her powers once channelized right can finally be the end of Drakaara.

Chapter 5: Drakaara

Before creation sang its first hymn, before the cosmos danced with the fires of the stars, there was a silence. A silence so profound it crushed the very possibility of life. Out of this void where nothingness reigned supreme was born **DRAKAARA.** Not in the brilliance of light but in the suffocating darkness that existed before time itself awoke.

Drakaara was the embodiment of Darkness itself-The first shadow that stirred when the universe dared to blink onto existence. Drakaara is not the silence of peace but the terror of an endless night. She was formed from the first whisper of nothingness, when the universe was still raw and chaotic. A dark flame in the depths of the abyss.

Her birth was not heralded by trumpets or waves of creation instead it was a slow awakening, a ripple in the deep well of the void. Where light sought to create, Drakaara sought to destroy. She is not a being made for the living, but one designed to reclaim all that dared to exist.

Drakaara rose from the void, her form elusive and ever-shifting. She was not born from the stars or the eclipse but from the very essence of darkness itself. Her eyes black as the void, shone with unnatural gleam- pits that reflected that reflects the emptiness that existed before existence. Her fingers long and pale extinguish stars with a mere touch, and where her footsteps fell, light itself fled.

Drakaara's existence was quiet a storm of destruction. While Eladarion crafted life and light across the galaxies, watching, waiting, she lingered in the folds of between those creations. Eladarion may have been born of the first light, but Drakaara- she was the first darkness and in her hands lays the end of everything for in her the universe sensed the inevitability of its own death.

As the first light of Eldarion sought to bathe the cosmos in its warmth, Drakaara Remained in the cold void, untouched, unyielding. Where Eldarion could only create, Drakaara understood the true nature of existence- Everything born of light must one day return to darkness-It was not hatred that drove her but an ancient understanding; light is fleeting but darkness is eternal. She was eternal.

It was then that she discovered her true purpose. As she moved through the empty corridors between galaxies, her hands reached out touching the stars. One by one, their light dimmed under her caress. But she did not snuff them out entirely-no that would be too simple. Instead she took their essence, their burning cores and trapped them within herself. Each star, each fragment of light she captured, was imprisoned in her growing collection, locked away in a cold dark place where time had no meaning.

Drakaara did not seek to destroy the universe outright: She sought to preserve its light in her own twisted ways. To her the galaxies were nothing more than fleeting flames, and she was the keeper of their final breath. She was the darkness that existed before creation and would be there long after it was gone.

Drakaara was more than a force of darkness-She was an artist, a creator in her own right. But unlike Eldarion who painted light and life. Her brush was dipped in the deepest blackness of the void. Her Canvas? The stars, the galaxies, the very fabrics of existence itself.

Her paintings were not mere representations. With each stroke she siphoned the life from celestial bodies-galaxies, stars, entire constellations, planets, Universes-Imprisoning their energy with the confines of her artwork. Planets that once spun in harmonious orbits were reduced to distant, frozen echoes, their light stolen, their warmth gone. When Drakaara painted, the universe wept. Entire solar systems would flicker and die, their essence devoured by her endless hunger.

She captured the violent birth of stars and silent death of black holes, locking them away in canvases that shimmered with dark magic. Each painting is a tomb, a creation suspended.

Drakaara, the embodiment of darkness, carriers an aura that is both haunting yet mesmerizing, reflecting her profound connection to the void from which she was born. Her appearance is a striking blend of ethereal beauty and chilling enigma, making her presence felt long before she is seen.

Her skin, an exquisite shade of obsidian, seems to absorb the very light around her giving her an almost spectral quality. It glistened like polished onyx under the faintest illumination, appearing both inviting and treacherous. Shadows play across her features emphasizing the sharp contours of her face-high cheekbones that rise like jagged cliffs in the night, and a jaw line that hints at both elegance and danger. Her lips, deep crimson are often curled into a slight knowing smile, as if she harbors secrets that are both alluring yet sinister.

Drakaara's hair cascades down her back in waves of midnight, shimmering with hints of deep purple and blue reminiscent of the endless cosmos flows like smoke, shifting and changing as if caught in an unseen wind and sometimes when she moves, it leaves a faint trail of dark, glittering stardust in its wake. Each strand appears to pulse with the energy of the captured stars she has imprisoned, a reminder of her endless hunger.

Her eyes are perhaps her most haunting feature-Void like and endless with irises that seem to swirl like galaxies caught in a vortex. They glow faintly, illuminated by the trapped energies of the stars she has consumed. When she gazes upon you, it feels as if she peers into your very soul, laying bare your fears and desires. In their depths lies the promise of oblivion, an invitation to embrace the darkness she embodies.

Drakaara's attire complements her dark essence. She drapes herself in flowing robes made from a fabric woven from shadows, the material shifting between shades of deep black and midnight blue. The robes are adorned with intricate patterns that resemble constellations, subtly glimmering as if the night sky has been stitched into her clothing. Each movement causes the fabric to ripple, creating an illusion that she is the darkness itself.

Around her neck hangs a pendant forged from the core of a long dead star, its brilliance trapped forever in a prison of dark energy. It pulses softly, a heartbeat of a stolen light and serves as both a talisman and reminder of the power she wields. Her fingers are adorned with rings made from the remnants of shattered worlds, each bearing a unique symbol-A tribute to the galaxies she has devoured.

Drakaara is not merely a sorceress, she is a living embodiment of the shadows and the silent force of that lies behind creation. Her look captivates and terrifies, a blend of beauty and horror that is unforgettable, marking her as the ancient artist who steals the very essence of existence to trap within her dark canvas.

Drakaara, the ancient sorceress and painter of darkness wields a formidable array of magical and supernatural powers that make her a fearsome force in the cosmos. Each power is a reflection off her essence- an embodiment of shadows, void and the primal force of creation through destruction. Her abilities not merely tools but extensions of her very being, allowing her to manipulate and mold existence itself.

Essence Absorption is one of Drakaara's most potent powers. With a mere touch, she can drain the life force and energies from stars, galaxies, celestial bodies. The moment she makes contact, their brilliance fades, leaving them cold and lifeless while she absorbs their essence into her own being or her paintings. This dark exchange not only strengthens her but also fuels her insatiable hunger for cosmic energy, making her more powerful with every celestial body she captures.

Accompanying this is the **Shadow Manipulation,** a power that grants her control over darkness itself. Drakaara can twist and shape shadows into tangible forms, creating illusions or solid constructs that can ensnare, suffocate or confuse her foes. These shadow tendrils can be shaped into lethal weapons or impenetrable barriers, allowing her to defend herself or strike with lethal precision. The darkness responds to her will, flowing like liquid night always at her command.

Another extraordinary ability is **Dimensional Travel,** which allows her to traverse the fabric of reality. Drakaara can slip between realms moving through the void- a realm devoid of light.

The chilling **Soul Binding** ability allows Drakaara to bind the souls of those she vanquishes, imprisoning them with her paintings. These tormented spirits become part of her dark collection, granting her insight into their experiences and emotions. Drakaara can summon these souls to serve as spies, soldiers or sources of information using their anguish to fuel her dark ambitions.

As a final display of her terrifying might she possesses **Reality Alteration** capabilities. With a brushstroke, Drakaara can reshape reality with the confines of her paintings. The scenes she creates spring to life, allowing her to trap enemies within alternate dimensions of design. These worlds reflect dual nature as a creator and destroyer.

Drakaara's grip on the psyche is equally formidable with her **Nightmare Induction** ability. She can invade the dreams of her victims, planting seeds of despair and fear that blossom into horrifying nightmares. By establishing a connection with their subconscious, she manipulates their dreams to reflect their deepest fears weakening them mentally and leaving them vulnerable to her influence. The nightmares become a weapon, eroding their resolve while she remains a haunting presence in their minds.

Additionally **Shape shifting** is one of her most intriguing powers. Drakaara can alter her physical form assuming the appearance of any being or creature she desires. This ability allows her to infiltrate enemy ranks or escape from dangerous situations by transforming into a more unassuming or fearsome figure.

Chapter 6: Forging Alliance

In the deepest corners of Ology, where ethereal **"Dreamweaver Flakes" floated** like whispers of the cosmos, Lunaara reveled in their sweet flavors-A delicate dance of moonlight and sweetness that filled her spirit with joy. The glade was aglow with soft luminescence, the air tinges with the vibrant energy of the surrounding "**Glitter bees"**-Tiny beings of light and laughter that wove happiness into the most sadistic of the hearts.

Suddenly, a burst of shimmering light broke the tranquility. The Astryn's emerged, their bodies glowing with vibrant hues, each step resonating with a melodic hum that echoed through the sacred grove. As they approached, the glitter bees swirled around them, their luminescence brightening the glade like a thousand twinkling stars.

Seeing them back only ignited flashback in the mind of Lunaara. Flash back of A an unpleasant encounter, flashbacks of a grave combat. Lunaara was about to launch its attack when she saw the Astryn's communicating with her.

Astryn 1: Warm amber pulsed in its body radiating sincerity and regret.

We regret our misunderstanding.

The air shimmered with their energy, illuminating Lunaara's surrounding with a Soft, inviting glow. She watched as the Astryn's bowed slightly, their diamond bodies bending with a grace that seemed to transcend the very fabric of reality.

Astryn 2: Soft waves of Pink and gentle whites radiating a soothing energy that washed over its body like a balm.

Joy can heal wounds.

Lunaara remained skeptical, her heart still guarded from the clash they had previously faced. The Astryn's approach this time was gentle. Their bodies shimmering with glowing colors, glowing with compassion.

Lunaara: Her body flickered with a bend of pale grey and silver reflecting her uncertainty and guardedness.

Why should I trust you? Especially after our last clash? Shadows linger between us.

Astryn 3: Its Diamond bodies now flickered with vibrant greens and gold illuminating it with urgency and hope.

We misunderstood your purpose. Let us share the truth with you. We come with clarity and purpose.

As Lunaara considered their plea the glitter bees danced around her, their laughter infusing the air with warmth and hope. She felt their joy seep her being, prompting her to lower her defenses.

The glade shimmered with energy as Lunaara shifted her stance curiosity beginning to overshadow her caution. The Astryn's sensing her change in mood radiated with colors of encouragement-Rich purples and bright yellows swirling around them like a vibrant aurora.

Astryn 1: Its body pulses with soft gold and shades of purple forming wave like patterns reaching out with tentative energy.

We recognize our mistake Lunaara and seek a bond, we want to be allies.

Feeling the sincerity of it plea, Lunaara's defenses fell further she stepped forward, cautious but filled with hope and uncertainty.

Lunaara: Its body now began to flicker in shimmering silver and muted blue making tiny spiral like patterns across its body.

What do you seek from me?

Astryn 1: Its body now starts to radiate in orange and vibrant greens slowly forming explosion of colors.

You are destined to confront the darkness that threatens us all. You are the key to our survival.

Lunaara: Its body now began to form random waves of rainbow colors across its body-A sign of confusion.

I fail to understand. I am confused.

Astryn 1: Its body now started to explode in radiant colors of orange, yellow and purple illustrating the balance of her being emphasizing the duality within her.

Your essence is unique, you are neither light not dark, you embody both. You are the bridge between two worlds.

The air shimmered with energy as Lunaara was trying to understand what the Astryn's had communicated to her. Her curiosity piqued by their words. She felt an undeniable connection forming a bridge spanning the gap between their realities.

Astryn 2: Its body now started to shimmer in deep crimson a stark warning resonating within their tones, creating a pattern of triangle highlighting the peril posed by Drakaara.

Drakaara-The essence of darkness cannot be defeated by light alone, it is too fragile.

Astryn 3: Its body pulsing with shimmering indigo, and maroon reflecting determination, their patterns weaving a tapestry of strength around them.

Your birth was a fusion of light and dark-Created to defeat Drakaara. The primordial evil, the sorceress who traps the energies of Stars, Galaxies, Universes and Constellations in her paintings.

Lunaara now felt the gravity of their proclamation sink in, like the first rays of dawn breaking over the horizon. She was a being born from the very essay of duality a harmonious blend of light and dark. Lunaara absorbed their light her mind racing with the implications. She could feel the weight of destiny pressing upon her, as if the universe itself was urging her to step into the light. She was feeling all of these when one of the Astryn's generated a new set of light passing through its body.

Astryn 1: Its body now pulsed with dark purple making a wave like patterns fading into dark red straight lines.

Darkness is ruled by Drakaara's will, but you…

Lunaara: Her body now glowed with greenish pink colors resembling uncertainty. Forming spiral patterns fading into dim yellow.

But how can I be sure of my strength? I have yet to fully grasp my powers.

Astryn 2: Its luminescence intertwined with vibrant yellows and oranges creating a swirling dance of light that enveloped her, encouraging her to believe.

Trust in the bond we forge, together we shall grow stronger together.

Lunaara's heart quickened, the flickers of self doubt slowly dissipating. She realized that her fears could be quelled by the camaraderie forming around her.

Astryn 3: The lights in its body brightened to a brilliant spectrum, pulsating with anticipation and excitement inviting her to join them.

It's time to awaken the power within you. Let us begin your training. Your Journey starts now.

With renewed determination, the Astryn's gathered around Lunaara, their colors intertwining like a living tapestry of light.

Astryn 1: Its body pulsed in soft yellows and whites inviting her to channel her energy.

Let us harness your essence. Focus on the light within.

Lunaara closed her eyes concentrating as the light within her began to swirl and Dance. The Asrtyn's mirrored her movements, their bodies shimmering with encouragement. She could feel their energy coalescing around her, and the weight of her potential surged within their core.

Astryn 2:Its body now exploded into fiery reds and deep blue's but this time The colors burst out into the air from its face, igniting the air with energy as its light along with the light of the other Astryn guide her through the process.

Merge our strengths; merge our lights, our colors. This will be your first step into the training.

As Lunaara concentrated harder she felt the warmth of their energies enveloping her, their vibrant hues mingling with their own. She now focused inwards allowing her feelings to guide her. The very source of generating the lights within her body. This was the mode of communication used by the Astryns as well. Light and pattern based. Memories flocked her mind: The beauty of Kolog, The vibrant laughter of the glitter bees, the taste of the Dreamweaver flakes. With every thought, the light within her pulsed more vibrantly, responding to the warmth of her emotions.

Suddenly she felt a surge of energy as her essence merged with the Astryns. A brilliant flash of violet, indigo, blue, green, yellow, orange, red, and maroon, gold, silver erupted from the guts to her mouth and right out of her mouth, illuminating the glade in a dazzling array of colors. The light danced and flickered, casting shadows that leaped and twirled around them, filling the grove with vibrant life.

She felt exhilarated, the bonds of unity strengthening around her. Each pulse of light represented their trust into each other.

All 3 Astryn's: Their bodies shimmered in vibrant oranges and pinks, signaling enthusiasm and encouragement.

We will start with Illumina Vortex, channel your essence and let your emotions guide the light.

An open mouthed Lunaara now nodded, her own light flickering in the shades of deep violet, a mix of nervousness and eagerness. She focused on the connection between them, drawing strength from their unwavering belief in her.

The Astryns too began to weave a complex pattern in the air, their colors merging in a dance of radiant hues that swirled around the pink skies of Kolog.

Lunaara closed her eyes, feeling the warmth of their combined energies envelop her. She reached deep within herself, recalling her dreams of a brighter future, the warmth of the glitter bees and the magic of Kolog.

With each thought, her light began to pulse more vividly, transforming into a brilliant display of colors.

As she concentrated her harder, she visualized her anxieties as dark swirling clouds. With a deep breath, she released them allowing them allowing the darkness within her to merge into the light. The transformation was instantaneous-A spectacular explosion of colors erupted from her illuminating the glade in a dazzling array of reds, greens and blues.

In that moment Lunaara felt an unbreakable bond with the Astryn's. Together they created a vibrant tapestry of light, each pulse resonating with hope and determination. The Illumina Vortex spun faster a whirlwind of colors spiraling outwards, resonating with the musical beats of the magical lands of Kolog.

With her hear still racing Lunaara concentrated harder than ever, her essence blending with theirs. The shield grew stronger, a radiant barrier that shimmered with power of their collective hope. But not everything was as hopeful in a star far far away from Kolog. A star named **CRYSTALLIUM.**

Chapter 7: Crystallium

Crystallium, a beacon of unmatched brilliance stood as one of the three brightest stars in the known universe. Suspended in the cosmic tapestry, it radiated a light so pure that even the most distant galaxies would pause to marvel at its glow. Unlike ordinary stars, crystallium was a living realm, a sanctuary of light and sound wove seamlessly. Its surface was a breathtaking expanse of crystalline plains, refracting the star's internal luminescence into rainbows that arched across the sky. Rivers of liquid known as **Star Essence** coursed through these paths, thrumming with the pulse of Crystallium's heart.

Every corner of Crystallium hummed with the life. The atmosphere resonated with an eternal song, a melody said to be the voice of the star itself. The skies were filled with constellation so bright they seemed to sing in harmony, joining the melody of the world below. Towering spires of quartz and prismatic gems reached skywards, their jagged peaks scattering beams of light into dazzling constellations. Forests of gem-encrusted trees, with leaves made of sapphire and diamond creating a chiming sound that complement the eternal song. Even the ground paved with opalescent stones, glistened as if kissed by the first light of creation.

The inhabitants of this radiant world, the **Crystal Vales** were beings of unmatched beauty and complexity. Composed of translucent mineral structures intertwined with living light, their forms shifted and gleamed with every emotion they felt. A crystal vale's body was a living spectrum: A glimmer of soft pink signified joy, while deep violets hinted at introspection. They communicated a language of notes and harmonies through symphonies of sound that resonated across their crystalline city **Glintoria.**

Glintoria was more than a city: It was the heart and soul of Crystallium. It stood as a sprawling metropolis of translucent towers that seemed woven from stardust itself, bridges spun from strands of crystal, and arches that shimmered with each passing note. Glintoria never knew darkness as its structure absorbed and refracted the star's light, creating a mesmerizing dance of colors that shifted with the inhabitant's emotions.

The symphony of Glitter was the core of Crystal Vale society. A sacred tradition that bound the beings to their star. This powerful song, when performed by the **Light keepers**-The most skilled and powerful of the Crystalvales-Channeled Crystallium's energy, creating protective aura's and vibrant beams capable of cutting through any darkness. The symphony could heal, illuminate and repel even the most potent shadows. When the song rose it did more than resonate through the city. It stirred the very core of Crystallium causing the rivers of star essence to shimmer more brightly and the gem leaved trees to sway as if in reverence.

The light keepers were the guardians of **Sparkly Heart**-A sacred core said to be a fragment of Eldarion's first light a relic that keeps crystallium alive. Tales whispered of the heart's power to renew life and banish even the darkest of the voids. The crystalvales believed that as long as the symphony was sung, crystallium would stand, its light undimmed by the voids of the universe.

Yet beneath the harmony, a subtle disquiet thrummed. Whispers communicated through melancholy notes and somber chords passed between the crystalvales. A rare tremor in the symphony would draw eyes skywards, hearts fluttering with shared apprehensions. They felt it-a distant shiver in the cosmos an echo of an ancient shadow they hoped would never touch Crystallium.

In the grand spires of Glintoria, the Light Keepers prepared for the unexpected, their bodies shimmering with anxious greens and sharp silvers. They rehearsed the symphony of glitter with renewed vigor the chords rising with fierce determination. Crystallium's glow never faltered but the choral skies seemed to hold their breath as if waiting for an approaching storm.

Beyond the edges of space, where the brightness of their star could not reach, a pair of void black eyes watched with cold anticipation. The air shimmered with a vibrant luminescence as Drakaara descended upon Crystallium. As Drakaara hovered above, her dark silhouette cast an ominous shadow over this sanctuary.

With a wave of her hand, she summoned **Dark Lights**-Patterns of pitch black energy that radiated from her core. These patterns flickered and twisted around her, shifting with her emotions communicating a language of Darkness which was universal.

Drakaara:A swirling vortex of dark triangles.

Let the hunt begin, my treasures.

As the patterns rippled through the air, the shadows darted across the landscape, creeping into every corner, siphoning the essence of Crystallium. Flowers that had bloomed in radiant colors wilted under the oppressive darkness, their hues fading to lifeless grays. Creatures once bursting with vitality froze in fear, drawn toward Drakaara like moths to flame. In response to the encroaching darkness the Light Workers rallied to defend their homes. **Aethyra**-Their leader emerged against the dark side.

Aethyra: A bright linear pulse cutting through the darkness making the shape of X from its core.

You invade sacred grounds.

Drakaara's laughter echoed like the shattering of glass, her dark patterns swirling ominously.

Drakaara: Sharp, Jagged jet black lines forming circles pulsated rhythmically.

Oh Aethyra your light only enriches my canvas. You are but brushstrokes in my grand masterpiece.

With a flick of her wrist, Drakaara unleashed a torrent of shadows, dark tendrils snaking towards the guardians. They fought valiantly their forms glowing brighter as they intertwined their energies into a brilliant shield. With fierce determination, the guardians and the light workers formed a barrier of stark white light pushing against the shadows that threatened to consume them. Drakaara sensing the surge of light retaliated with a Dark Vortex, aiming to overwhelming their brilliant shield. But the guardians and the light workers pressed on, their colors intertwining in a mesmerizing display.

In the heart of the chaos, Crystal Vales fought back-A vibrant testament to resilience –refusing to become a mere brushstroke in Drakaara's dark design.

The light workers now began assembled together and began to draw shockwaves of light which was then aimed at Drakaara. Causing waves of radiant energy crash Drakaara. Each pulse of Light intertwined with the harmonious essence of Crystallium, creating a dazzling display that illuminated the dark sky.

The impact sent shockwaves rippling across crystaalium scattering shimmering shards of crystal that sparkled like stars in the dimming light. Aethyra and her fellow guardians pressed on weaving intricate spells of protection that manifested as radiant barriers against this encroaching darkness.

As a battle intensified, the guardians moved in perfect harmony, creating intricate formations that dazzled the eye. Crystalline creatures, born of the valley's magic joined the fight, their bodies reflecting light in a myriad of hues. They swirled around Drakaara, creating a mesmerizing spectacle drifting her from the assault. Drakaara's eye narrowed, fury igniting within her. With a fierce gesture, she unleashed a tempest of shadows, dark tendrils snaking through the air and snatching at the guardians, light workers and ordinary citizen of crystalvales using shadow manipulation. The ethereal beings dodged and weaved, their luminous forms dancing gracefully in the encroaching darkness.

The battlefield transformed into a magnificent maelstrom of light and dark. Aethrya channeled her strength, summoned the heart of crystallium-a colossal crystal that pulsed with the collective energy of the CrystalVales. The crystalvales now emitted a blinding light a last stand against the encroacher. The crystal's light surged forth, a beacon of hope illuminating the dark storm. Drakaara faltered momentarily blinded by the brilliance. Seizing the moment, the guardians unleashed a final barrage of small pinkish purple bombs resembling plasma bombs striking at the heart of the Darkness. But Drakaara quickly regained her composure. The very air thickened with tension as she conjured the shadows drawing energy from the very essence of the Crsytallium.

One by one the guardians, the light workers, the crystal vales fell back their energy warning under the relentless assault of Darkness. Aethyra's voice trembled as he summoned the last of his strength but the shadows engulfed him snatching away the brilliance he had fought to protect. Drakaara wields her paintbrush not on canvas but on the atmosphere of Crystallium itself. Her process of capturing stars, galaxies, planet, and constellations is a mesmerizing ritual. One that draws on the raw magic of creation.

Her brush crafted from a dark mixture of Supernova, Ashes and Bones is dipped into a spectral pool of black liquid, with a graceful movement of hands uttering ancient spells she draws in threads of starlight and weaves them onto her cosmic canvas. As she paints every crystalvale, every light worker, every guardian materializes into her strokes, burning and spinning as if alive. With a flick of her wrist the symphony of glitter and the sparkly heart-The very core of Crystallium keeping it alive swirl into her cosmic canvas carrying with them the entire life force of crystallium screaming for help, still glowing with life. And that is when she isolates the sparkly heart and merges it with her dark magical robe which was made from the shadows making it a part of her.

As her work in Crystallium is done, her new painting glows with the lights of countless crystal vales, each one captured in eternal darkness. Drakaara then breathes across the canvas, sealing it and in that breath; the painting became a self containing reality. With that she turned her gaze towards **"Emrithar-The second brightest star in the universe."**

Chapter 8: Emrithar

Emithra hung in the vast canvas of the cosmos like a dream, glowing with a richness that defied mortal comprehension. It was not just a star but a realm woven from emerald and magic, a world within itself. Far from the ordinary spheres of fire and gas, Emithra pulsed with a living energy, its brilliance a beacon of mystery and allure. Those who beheld it from afar could scarcely believe its reality: Its green light shimmered like a precious jewel but radiated with a force that seemed to whisper, to call out to distant souls with a timeless wisdom.

The surface of Emithra was no simple terrain it was a world of verdant wonder, filled with vast crystalline fields that stretched into infinity. Fields of emerald blades, taller than any tree and razor-sharp grew in winds that carrier not air but pure magic, a ceaseless breeze of enchantment. Each blade glistened with a thousand shades of green and when they swayed, they caught the light and split it into iridescent shards, creating a mesmerizing dance of colors across the vast expanse of Emithra's surface.

Beneath these emerald plains ran rivers but not of water. The streams of Emithra were radiant green substances known as Aetherflow winding through the land like veins of molten emerald. The rivers glowed faintly, casting a gentle green radiance on everything they touched, nourishing the land with pulsating energy. Their currents moved with an unpredictable rhythm, shifting in response to celestial alignments and sometimes flowing upwards, defying gravity as if obeying a mystical pattern. At certain times the rivers would spiral up and meet, forming temporary portals above the surface, a gateway only visible to the purest souls. Legends told of beings, who crossed the portals and returned touched by Emithra's light forever altered. Above this strange, enchanted landscape hung luminous clouds that were themselves composed of emerald dust. These clouds filled with dense magical vapors were known to crystallize and drift down like snow, coating the ground with a soft, glowing sheen. These dust falls created fleeting pathways that lit up with every step and stories told of ancient beings who once walked these glowing traits, leaving footprints that still shimmered.

Ye the true wonder of Emithra laid beneath its surface. The soil was infused with wellsprings, pooling in underground caverns as emerald-hued lakes, their surfaces so still they mirrored the heavens themselves. These lakes were more than mere reflections: They were portals, windows into other realms and distant stars. Beings of great wisdom often came to these lakes, seeking visions and answers that even the universe seemed hesitant to reveal. A single drop from these lakes if carried was rumored to grant knowledge beyond imagining a secret that only the oldest stars understood.

And there were the creatures-The guardians of Emithra. Ethereal beings made of emerald and light known as the Erthyrians, they glided silently above the star's surface. Their forms were graceful, vaguely humanoid yet ever shifting with limbs that appeared to be forged from pure energy, casting trails of green fire behind them. They were the protectors, defenders of Emithra's magic and their gaze was sharp as the blades that grew from the star's soil. It was believed they could sense even the slightest disturbance in the magical fabric of Emithra and when they moved, the air hummed with power, echoing the song of the star.

Emithra was not merely a star but a kingdom of wonder, life and mystery, a realm where every element thrummed with enchantment. Here force was the very essence of existence an eternal dance of light, color and energy. Emithra's green glow continued to pulse through the cosmos, a jewel in the fabric of the universe a jewel that few could reach and fewer still could understand.

It began as a whisper, a subtle tremor that rippled through the very core of Emithra. The lifeblood of the star, a vast gleaming expanse of emerald plains and crystalline forests- Began to flicker, its vibrant glow diming as if overtaken by an unseen shadow. The Erythrians with their delicate forms woven from pure starlight felt the disturbance immediately. Their silvery bodies trembled, dimming as though an invisible hand had begun to siphon away their very essence. In a single, shivering moment a chill swept across Emithra, darkening the air, the rivers, and even the skies above.

And then she arrived.

Drakaara descended upon Emithra with the weight of a curse, her very presence casting a shroud over a once-bright landscape. A figure wreathed in swirling shadows, she moved with a cold predatory grace. Her eyes glinting with an insatiable hunger as they swept over Emithra's treasures. With a slow deliberate gesture, Drakaara raised her hands, and tendrils of Darkness slithered from her fingertips like snakes coiling and twisting as they stretched towards Emithra. The tendrils snaked through the emerald forests, wrapping around every tree, every blade of shimmering grass, pulling the land's essence into the shadowy depths of her form. She was a parasite, drawing the life and wonder from Emithra, her tendrils burrowing deep, sapping every drop of the star light. Her shadows enveloped everything she touched, reducing vibrant landscapes to withered husks, leaving nothing but hollow echoes of their former beauty. The rivers of light once flowing with crystalline purity now turned stagnant and black. As her shadows stretched across the land, Drakaara's painting-a dark canvas that she had carried with her began to pulsate, drawing in the stolen magic capturing every flicker of Emithra's essence. The painting absorbed the land's life, its once-vibrant colors bleeding into dark strokes and twisted patterns, each brushstroke a symbol of her conquest. With every inch of ground her shadows consumed, the canvas grew darker, richer, feeding off Emithra's energy, transforming it into her own dark masterpiece.

But Emithra was not a star to surrender its life so easily. From the very heart of its Emerald's glow a deep ancient power surged-A final rallying cry that echoed through Erythrian soul. The luminous beings, bound by their love for their homeland, gathering in defiance, their united light blazing brighter than ever before. The **Gemlocks,** towering protectors with bodies of emerald crystal planted themselves forming a wall of green fire. Above them the **Sky dancers** dove in synchronized arcs, their wings casting showers of stardust that seemed to ignite the very air. With a gesture of command, the **Elder Erythrian** raised his staff high, a surge of emerald energy blasted through the land, bolstering every tree and every tree and every gust of air attacking Drakaara.

Drakaara's face now twisted in an amused smile, but a hint of annoyance flickered in her eyes. She raised her hand and from her cosmic canvas, a horde of shadowy creatures poured forth-twisted beasts with claws of obsidian and eyes that burned with soulless hunger. The dark entities charged, crashing against the wall of emerald light with a land shaking impact. Yet the Erythrians held their ground, their combined energy blasting through drakaara's creatures, shattering them into dust. The gemlocks surged forward, their fists like hammer, crushing the shadows that dared to approach. Their movements were swift and coordinated ringing like a chime that resonated across Emithra.

But Drakaara was not so easily deterred. She clenched her fist, and from her canvas waves of pure shadow erupted, swallowing the land in a suffocating darkness. The Erythrians felt the pressure building around them, their light beginning to waver. The Elder Erythrian's face was drawn and weary, but he did not falter. He called upon the sacred crystal vines of Emithra-ancient tendrils that had slept beneath the star's surface for eons. They burst from the ground in spirals of Gleaming green, lashing out towards Drakaara with a force born of despair. The vines struck with blinding speed, coiling around Drakaara's shadows, binding them in a trap woven from the very heart of Emithra. The Erythrians cheered, their voices lifted in hopeful defiance. The skydancers attempted a final dive, their wings blazing with the last of their strength as Drakaara's shadows swarmed around them, the elder Erythrian channeled Emithra's very core, sending a beam of emerald light straight at Drakaara's canvas. The beam struck with such force that it split the ground, its glow blinding in its intensity. Hope flickered around them against Drakaara's darkness. But Drakaara relentless and unyielding raised both hands, summoning **Dark Bombs-** Jet black bombs which suck the energy of its target. Aiming right at the Elder Erythrian. The elder fell to his knees like a dying ember, his life draining its heartbeat slowing to a final, echoing pulse. With a triumphant smile, Drakaara drew all of Emithra's energy, light and life into her cosmic canvas. The vibrant star that had once been a beacon in the universe was now trapped, its beauty and power came to a standstill. The battlefield fell silent, a desolate void where life and light had once thrived.

Drakaara looked down at her completed workman twisted canvas brimming with the essence of Emithra. She ran her fingers over it, feeling the captured magic pulsing beneath the surface, a testament to her victory. She now moved forward to the depths of Emithra where **Valkyra-** A bright greenish yellow stone was still glowing with pulsating energy. Valkyra was the heart of Emithra. The origin stone of all light, life and wonder of Emithra. Drakaara now approached Valkyra and that is when she isolates it and merges it with her dark magical robe which was made from the shadows making it a part of her. Drakaara then breathes across the canvas, sealing it and in that breath; the painting became a self containing reality.

Drakaara now using her shadow manipulation merges both sparkly heart and Valkyra into a semi tangible jet black like structure which looks like a pole. She now thinks "Two Down, just one more to go"

With that she turned her gaze towards **"Pulsitar-The third brightest star in the universe."**

With a final glance at the void she had created, Drakaara set her sights on her next target, her shadow now fading into the Darkness as Emithra the once-brilliant star now remained only as echo with her cosmic prison.

Chapter-9: Pulsitar

Pulsitar-The last of the brightest stars in the universe, its radiant glow piercing through the cosmic void, brighter and more mysterious than any other celestial body. It was not merely a star-It was a living, breathing phenomenon forged from the perfect convergence of neutron matter and plasma. It pulse with energy so pure and intense that it could distort the fabric of space itself. At its core was an unimaginably dense heart-A massive cluster of neutron matter that tugged at the very thread of existence, its force so great that it bent light and warped time The star's outer layer of plasma glowed in hues no living being could truly describe-shifting, fluid and ethereal. Pulsitar's magnetic fields, drawn from its intense energy, wove through the plasma like invisible threads, interacting with the universe itself, bending light in their wake. It was the heartbeat of the cosmos, and everything within its reach felt the reverberations of its power.

From the heart of this vast, living star emerged the **PULSAR'S-** being of Pulsitar's very essence. They were creatures of pure energy, their forms not made of solid matter but of radiant, shifting plasma. No two pulsars were alike: Their shapes were ever-fluid constantly changing in tune with the rhythms of their star. One moment they would appear as elegant tendrils of light, twisting and spiraling in delicate arcs: The next they would coalesce into vast shimmering waves of energy, their forms as fluid as the plasma they were made of.

The Pulsars had no fixed bodies- they were more like living patterns of energy, existence in a state of constant flux. Each Pulsars existence was intimately tied to Pulsar itself. They thrived in the ever-changing currents of the star's plasma; their movements synchronized the pulse of the star. They were not bound by the limitations solid forms but flowed with the star's rhythm, part of its very being. Their connection to Pulsitar was sacred-Its pulse was their heartbeat, its plasma their sustenance, without Pulsitar they could not exist. They were not solitary beings. They live in a community, of network of interconnected light formed the foundation of their civilization. Their city **ZEPHARIEL** was a city of pure, radiant energy. It was city of light, a city of perpetual motion. Its structures were formed from radiant threads of energy that glowed softly. The city was both beautiful and functional. Great spires of crystalline energy reached towards the sky. Streets and pathways of flowing plasma crisscrossed the city winding like rivers of light that changed and evolved with every moment. The atmosphere of Zephariel was alive and humming with energy, as the very air seemed to vibrate with the rhythms of Pulsitar.

The Pulsars were deeply spiritual beings, revering Pulsitar as the source as the source of all life and energy. They understood that their existence was part of the star's pulse that they were born from energy and would eventually turn to it. They saw themselves as stewards of Pulsitar, guardians of its flow, protectors of the delicate balance that sustained their world. The star's pulse was not just a source of power: It was a sacred rhythm that guided their lives.

In the heart of Zephariel, a magnificent structure stood, the **Crystalis Nexus,** a vast, crystalline dome that houses the pulse chamber. This was where the Pulsars gathered to meditate, to commune with the stars, and to connect with deep harmonic frequencies that pulsar emitted within the pulse chamber, they would lose themselves in the rhythms of the star, entering a state of heightened awareness, where their consciousness merged with the pulse of the universe itself. The Pulsars had studied the cosmos for eons, learning the secrets of energy, light and the very fabric of the universe. They had unlocked the mysteries of Pulsitar's plasma currents and had mastered the art of harnessing energy from the start itself. With this knowledge they had created technologies-light based constructs and energy-weaving tools- that allowed them to manipulate their environment, to shape the plasma flows around them and to build structures from the very light that surrounded them. It was a world of harmony and balance, where every pulse of energy, every shift of light had meaning. The pulsars lived in prefect synchrony with their star, their existence a dance of light and energy.

The harmonious pulse of Pulsitar reverberated through Zaphariel each beat of its rhythm a reminder of the delicate balance the Pulsars maintained with their star. Life in the city was a seamless flow of light energy, and purpose, a world where the very air shimmered with a constant hum of celestial power. But beneath the beauty and order of this radiant existence, something dark was stirring-A shadow creeping silently across the cosmos, one that threatened to unweave the very fabric of this peaceful world.

In the distance, beyond the shimmering city of Zaphariel, the sky flickered. It was faint at first, a subtle disruption in the constant harmonious glow that enveloped Pulsitar. At first no one took notice-what was but a tiny rift in the flow of energy? A speck in the vastness of their reality? But as the pulses of light began to distort, a deeper, unnatural vibration rippled through the very core of Pulsitar. The star once stable and constant began to tremble under the weight of a foreign presence. It was as though the rhythm, of the universe itself was being silence by an alien force a presence that was not welcomed here.

From the void appeared-Drakaara.

Her eyes were now set on this radiant star, the third brightest star in the universe. She descended upon Pulsitar like a collapsing black hole, an inescapable gravity that wrapped space and light around her. As Drakaara approached the flow of Pulsitar's plasma began to sputter, as if gasping for air. The magnetic fields once steady and unyielding began to tremble in the face of her power. The radiant glow that had once illuminated Zephariel began to flicker, dimming with each passing moment.

The pulsars once peaceful and in tune with their star's pulse began to stir uneasily. Their energy patterns once harmonious now flickered erratically as the first whispers of fear took hold. Something was wrong. The star's pulse was being smothered and worse they could feel the life with Pulsitar the very essence of the star's existence being drawn inward swallowed by an unseen force.

With a surge of unnatural power, Drakaara's dark tendrils reached out latching onto the heart of the star. Pulsar's groaned, the very core of their being feeling the pressure of Drakaara's hunger. The pulsars bound to the star by their very nature, felt the sharp pangs of their distress. They knew instinctively what was happening: The star was being devoured. The very energy that sustained their world. Their lives were being sucked into an abyss from which it would never return. The Pulsars reacted with urgency, they were not warriors but they were beings of energy-Powerful in their own right, connected deeply to the essence of Pulsitar. They converged in the center of Zephariel their forms glowing brighter as they began to weave their collective energy into a shield around the star. Light clashed with darkness as the Pulsars tried to push back against the force of Drakaara's invasion, their energy rippling outward in an attempt to stem the flow of her consuming void.

But Drakaara was relentless, with a wave of her dark tendrils; she tore through the Pulsar's defenses, unraveling their light with ease. The Pulsar's screamed-Not in pain, but in the resonance of their energy being ripped apart. The entire city of Zephariel trembled as the very foundation of their world was shaken by the force of Drakaara's attack. The arrival of Drakaara was like ink spilled across stardust, a darkness that absorbed every glimmer. She moved through the galaxy, drawn to Pulsitar's rare light.

The Pulsars rose to defend their home, their luminous forms casting rays that shot through the space around them. In unison, they chanted a phrase, a plea and command, ancient words imbued with very essence of Pulsitar: **LUX CAELUM MIHI VIRES DEDIT ME SEQUERE.** Their chants called forth radiant shields and glowing weapons firmed from the essence of the star itself, threads of stardust winding together to create barriers strong enough to hold against any force- or so they believed. Drakaara merely watched a smirk hidden within the shifting shadows that cloaked her. She extended her hand, fingers trailing through the cosmic dust, summoning dark wisps that spiraled outwards like tendrils of liquid night. The pulsar's radiant shields woven from Pulsitar's own starlight each one reflecting the dazzling hues of their star. But Drakaara's tendrils slipped through the light, snaking around the shields and splitting them like glass, shard scattering the void as the Pulsar's defenses crumbled.

The Pulsars retaliated with a storm of enchanted light. A dozen beams each with the intensity of a new born star, blazed toward her converging with a force that could have melted planets. But drakaara was undeterred: She raised her blackened brush and with a flick redirected the light. In her gasp the blazing beams transformed into a thousand strands of starlit ink, twisting into intricate patterns that melded with her canvas. Every stroked pulled more of Pulsitar's magic into her masterpiece, as if the very essence of the star was drawn into the threads of her painting.

The Pulsars called upon every spell they knew, each a spark of ancient magic. Trails of shimmering silver wrapped around her, attempting to bind her movements. **MAELLOR- the eldest of the Pulsars** summoned a spiral of luminous mist that morphed into a massive creature, a celestial serpent that lunged toward Drakaara with fangs of crystal light. But Drakaara was prepared: She dipped her brush into the darkness and swirled it in a graceful arc. Her strokes twisted the mist and the creature into a vortex, trapping it in a whirl of Darkness, its brilliance dimming as it became yet another of her cosmic design.

Maellor now gathered his kin with a single nod, his form pulsating with an aura of resolve. The Pulsars circled around Drakaara, linking their energies to create a protective ring around Pulsitar, amplifying their combined magic until the starlit ring blazed like a miniature sun. They chanted ancient words, calling on the primal magic of the cosmos, and the space around Drakaara shimmered with traps woven from the strands of pure light. Shimmering nets formed in every direction, each line laced with shards of Pulsitar's essence they closed in, binding her form and siphoning her strength back towards the star.

Drakaara paused, caught for a moment in the glow of their celestial cape, her brush held motionless. But with a slow, deliberate movement, she dipped the tip into the heart of her shadow and swirled it through the binding light. The nets disintegrated into particles, each fragment a silver of Pulsar's magic and as they scattered she redirected the luminous energy, wrapping it around her painting like a frame. The Pulsar's chants faltered as their magic was absorbed into her canvas, the lines of light now snaking across her artwork in haunting patterns that pulsed with their fading essence.

In a final act of defiance, Maellor conjured a blade of crystallized stardust, each edge sharpened with fragments of his own light. Holding it aloft, he whispered a wordless plea to Pulsitar and the blade grew brighter humming with the pulse of the star itself. Maellor lunged at Drakaara, his form trailing light an unstoppable force of brilliance, But Drakaar's brush flashed once, twice, thrice in rapid succession, each stroke slicking through his attack. The blade shattered mid-air, dissolving into a thousand glimmers that fell like stardust around them. She then lifted her brush high and with a sweeping stroke she captured the essence of Pulsars siphoning their remaining light into the folds of her painting. Their glow dimmed, each Pulsar now bound in spectral stasis within the canvas, their expressions frozen in defiant awe. Maellor's light flickered once, twice and then faded, his form dissolving into the shadows that coiled around the brush. Finally Drakaara turned her gaze to Pulsitar itself the once blazing star now struggling to hold on to its own light. Her brush hovered in the cosmic silence, and then dipped down catching the last pulse of energy that rippled through the star. With deliberate strokes she painted the final traces of life, light and magic from Pulsitar. Capturing its essence entirely. The star's glow dimmed until it was nothing more than a faint, distant memory, bound forever in the folds of Drakaara's dark masterpiece. Drakaara then breathes across the canvas, sealing it and in that breath; the painting became a self containing reality.

Drakaara now capturing Pulsitar's essence now had begun to mold these stolen energies in what looked like a staff, a pole of darkness.

The Shadow Pole.

Chapter 10: Prelude to Darkness

Back at Kolog, Lunaara stood with her arms raised, her focus sharpened. The Astryn's circled her, their light patterns weaving in and out, guiding her through the complex dance of magic she was struggling to master. It was no longer about controlling the raw power within her, but understanding it-feeling the subtle currents of energy, waiting to be shaped.

She had come a long way since her first lesson, but this was different. The energy within her no longer obeyed simple commands: it was alive, wild and it pushed against the limits she tried to impose. With every breath, it swelled a surged, as though testing her resolve. She clenched her paws, trying to harness the force.

The nearest Astryn to her signaled-Its diamond body shimmering to a soothing pale blue leading to a pattern of white circles.

Calm your mind, Lunaara.

Lunaara exhaled slowly, trying to match the Astryn's rhythm. She felt the pulse of the land beneath her feet, the whisper of the wind through the inverted trees. Everything seemed to be singing in unison. Her mind stilled for a moment, and with it, the magic within her began to settle. The wild surge calmed, but it was still waiting, coiling under her skin.

The Astryns increased the temp of the movements. Their patterns shifted in flashes, light intertwining each one sending subtle bursts of energy toward her. Lunaara could feel their presence not as separate beings but as extensions of the world around her. They were teaching her not just to control her powers but to become one with it.

Another Astryn stepped forward its light forming a pattern of soft, warm gold triangles.

Focus on the flow, Feel it within you become the current not the dam.

She nodded trying to surrender to the sensation. She closed her eyes, letting go of her control for a moment, letting her light and darkness combined pulse through her. The wild surge within her began to calm, the storm becoming a gentle wave. Just as she began to feel the connection, a deep tremor rattled through the ground beneath them. Lunaara opened her eyes, and the Astryn's immediately froze, their light flickering in alarm.

The Astryn's exchanged urgent light patterns through their bodies in a sudden spiked fashion. This disturbance was unlike anything she had sensed before. It was at a distance from her but so powerful it felt as if it were right next to them.

The training session halted the gentle hum of magic turning into a sharp buzz. Lunaara's pulse quickened. What was this new force? And why was it disturbing?

She was thinking all these when it happened. A violent tremor, sudden and unrelenting, shook the Astryns. Their lights now flickered in a random manner, their bodies usually so steady and composed, shuddered and twisted in unnatural directions. A blinding burst of colors expanded within their body's lavenders, blues and purples clashing with violent reds and blacks. Their essence became jagged.

Lunaara stepped back instinctively a knot of anxiety twisting in her chest. The Astryn's trembling had intensified. Their once-perfectly synchronized light was now fractured, wild, as if the cosmic winds themselves had begun to howl tearing apart their calm, peaceful demeanor. For a moment her heart pounded in her chest, sensing that something had irrevocably shifted. Her eyes narrowed as she watched the Astryn's struggle, their forms shaking violently, light patterns splintering in a chaotic dance, she failed to understand was this a part of her training? Was this another cosmic trial she was meant to endure?

Without warning Lunaara's breath was caught as a new image flooded her senses too, too vivid, too real to be mere imagination. Drakaara the sorceress stood, her silhouette etched in shadows so thick they seemed to bleed into the very stars around her. She was no longer merely a sorceress-She was something more, something ancient and fearsome.

Drakaara raised her hand, and Lunaara's eyes followed her gaze, tracing the trajectory of her outstretched fingers towards a trio of stars in the distance. Crystallium, Emithra and Pulsitar. With a single flick of her wrist, she sucked all their life, light, wonder and energies in her cosmic canvas. The 3 brightest stars of the universe, the stars once untouched began to fade their brilliance stolen in an agonizing silence. Lunaara's stomach twisted. It was as if the light of the universe itself was drained. She could feel it every pulse, every flicker of energy being ripped from the stars, pulled into the cosmic canvas of Drakaara.

Lunaara watched horrified as Drakaara was molding the stolen energies into what looked like a staff, like a weapon of darkness-The Shadow Pole.

It shimmered with black glitter, a jet black rod that radiated with an eerie glow. The very air around it seemed to grow colder, denser. The shadow pole was unlike anything Lunaara had seen. It pulsed with a terrible, unnatural rhythm, a constant, insidious sucking force that seemed to draw everything in it-The light, life, wonder, energy all of it.

Drakaara raised the pole, the shadows clinging to it like a cloak, swirling around it in an otherworldly dance. Lunaara felt her breath freeze in her chest as the magnitude of the pole's power. It became clear if this weapon were to be placed in the center of the **Cosmic Wrap-**The birthplace of everything-It would drain all the light, all the life, all the magic from the universe. The stars, the planets, the very fabric of existence itself would be sucked into the void, consumed by the darkness of the shadow pole.

And that was the very intent.

Drakaara's laughter, cold and cruel, echoed through the vision, a sound that seemed to reverberate through every corner of the universe. Lunaara could see it now-Drakaara's plan. She wishes to capture all light, life, wonder, magic and energy of the universe. She would be the painter of a new universe, not with colors, but with stolen essence of life itself.

Then the visions faded but the implications remained. The universe was in grave danger, and Drakaara's reach was growing. Lunaara could feel the weight of her next choice pressing down on her was she ready to confront this Darkness? And could she trust the Astryn's to help her or had they too fallen victim to the shadows?

One of the Astryn's stepped forward, its form shimmering with a deep red hue. A grave almost sorrowful energy radiated from

within it. And Lunaara instinctively took a step back, it was clear that whatever had just happened, it was beyond their control.

Lunaara's heart raced her body shimmering with patterns of deep violets forming rectangles followed by waves of crimson.

What is it? What's happening?

The Astryn's light shifted again, turning to a somber violet and patterns began to form images of something dreadful unfolding in the distant reaches of the cosmos.

Drakaara has begun the creation of the Shadow Pole.

Lunaara's brow furrowed, her body began to glow with fluorescent yellows forming webs of spirals.

I fail to understand what is the Shadow Pole?

The Astryn's light flickered as if gathering their thoughts. Then with a quick sharp motion, the light painted an image but this time the image was released out in the air. The image was of a dark, towering pole, and its surface black as night, gleaming with particles like that of a dying star.

Astryn 1:Its began to flicker in pink and green forming waves which eventually turned into straight lines but this continued about 10 times until it stopped.

The Shadow Pole is forged from the life, light and magic of Crytallium, Emithra and Pulsitar 3 of the brightest stars in the universe.

Astryn 2: Its body now began to flicker with waves of orange, yellow and red but these waves were broken in parts. When suddenly these colors began to merge in a random, violent manner.

If the shadow pole is placed in the center of the Cosmic Wrap- The very fabric of existence, it will absorb all light, life and magic from the universe, trapping them within its core. The universe will fall into eternal darkness.

Lunaara's light flickered slowly making patterns of twisted lines of Silver and Gold and sometimes mixed.

She, she's going to destroy everything?

Lunaara was now barely able to process the magnitude of the threat.

Astryn 3: The indigo light in its body made patterns of huge sea waves which eventually turned into straight white lines.

Drakaara doesn't believe in destroying but capturing. The shadow pole is a masterpiece. A creation to capture all light and life of the universe.

Lunaara's body now began to making random lines of soft warm oranges.

So how do we stop her?

All Astryn's now stepped 2 inches closer to Lunaara. Their bodies now making circles of shades of soothing green and whites.

Lunaara now stood frozen, the images of Drakaara still lingering in her mind. The enormity of the task before her seemed impossible. Drakaara had stolen the light from three of the brightest stars of the universe and now this weapon-The shadow Pole would plunge everything into eternal darkness.

Lunaara's lights within her body now began to falter as she tried to control the random patterns they were forming. After a current of random patterns she finally controlled her light in shades of light blue and purple forming triangular waves like pyramids.

How can I stop something like that? How can I even stand against a sheer raw power of nature like her?

The Astryn's lights swirled gently their patterns calming but still tinged with a deep sorrowful glow of violet, maroon and crimson.

You are the answer Lunaara, the power within you is the answer to Drakaara. But to face her you must first face yourself. The power of the shadow pole will only be undone by the light which resides within you alongside the darkness. Lunaara's heart races as she absorbed their light and patterns. The path ahead was clear. But the journey felt like a leap into the unknown. There was no certainty, no guarantee of success but one thing was undeniable-She could not fail for if she did the universe would fall into oblivion.

She clenched her fists, feeling the pulse of energy within her once more, the storm that was yet to be tamed. With the Astryns by her side she had no choice but to push forward.

Lunaara's body now radiated with lights of warm silver and yellow making an intricate pattern of tiny star like designs but not exactly stars.

What must I do?

The Astryns's now frightened began radiating pitch red lights from their bodies forming a pattern which looked like a constellation never seen before.

Head to Cosmic Wrap and prevent Drakaara from inserting the Shadow Pole in the middle of it, these are the co-ordinates for it and do not worry for we will join you.

Chapter 11: Cosmic Wrap

In the boundless expense of the void, where the known universe frays into an endless sea of shadows, lies the **Cosmic Wrap,** Veiled in an aura of raw, unbridled magic. It is no ordinary place for it is the cradle of existence, a shimmering nexus where light, life, energy and magic were born. Pulsating with an ethereal radiance, the cosmic wrap glows like a living tapestry, its thread spun from the purest elements of creations. To gaze upon it is to glimpse the universe's soul, a sight so overwhelming that even the most ancient of beings would bow in reverence.

The wrap does not merely exist-It breathes. Waves of light ripple across its surface, forming intricate ever-changing patterns that seem to hum with the first vibrations of creation. These patterns are not random: They tell tales of stars igniting, galaxies blooming like cosmic flowers. The air or rather the space around it-thrums with an energy so profound that it bends reality, pulling the very fabric of the cosmos inwards like an eternal heartbeat.

Surrounding the wrap is **KAELYON Constellation**, a collection of stars that form an impossibly intricate lattice. Each star glimmers with a unique hue, casting prismatic beams that converge upon the wrap as if offering tribute to its majesty. Legends say these stars were the first to be born, their light sculpted directly from the wrap's core. Their alignment is ever-changing shifting to guard the cosmic wrap from those unworthy of its powers. This celestial ballet has confounded even the Astryn's whose knowledge of the universe is unparalleled.

The cosmic wrap itself is not a place one can simply enter it is alive, conscious and selective only those deemed worthy by its ancient essence may pass through its luminescent veil. To others, it appears as an impenetrable sphere of light, its surface reflecting their deepest fears and desires. The unworthy who attempt to force their way in are said to dissolve into stardust, their essence absorbed to fuel the wrap's eternal glow.

But for those who dare and succeed, the wrap's interior is a realm unlike any other-A landscape of infinite potential where streams of liquid light flow like rivers and crystalline structures hum with the frequency of creation. It is here that the source of all existence resides. A radiant core of pure energy that pulses with intensity so fierce it can illuminate entire galaxies. To touch it, to wield it, to command the very essence of the cosmos. But such power comes with a price-One that no being has ever been willing to pay.

Under the cascading brilliance of Kolog's Rainbow Falls the Astryns and Lunaara gathered in tense determination. The air itself hums with an unspoken urgency, each sound echoing the weight of their mission, beneath them the musical lands hum softly, the tones rising with each droplet of the rainbow colored rains.

One Astryn stands at the center, its triangular face radiating a steady golden light that pulses with authority. Streams of patterns ripple outwards from its glow weaving through the space between them. The meaning is clear: Their path to Cosmic Wrap must be forged quickly.

Gold streaks flare into angular bursts of crimson followed by golden lights weaving into intricate sequences resembling the stars of the universe.

The constellation will not yield easily. Its stars guard the wrap with riddles of ancient light. If Drakaara reaches it before us creation will fall into darkness.

Another Astryn floats forward, its form shimmering with silvers and blues, its light calm yet resolute.

Making spirals of soft blues which intensifies leading into streaks of silver into shapes of U.

The only way to breach the Kaelyon constellation's defense is to fold space upon itself. A gateway formed by our collective essence. But we cannot stabilize it alone. Lunaara's power will be the anchor. The only force strong enough to withstand the wrap's pulls.

At the heart of their gathering Lunaara's form glows with a deep violet radiance, forming measured pulses. **Her light shifts into deep indigo which then fades into a steady green.**

I will anchor the bridge conveying her resolve.

One Astryn's crimson tinged light flickers erratically, though it quickly masks itself in muted tones of gray projecting an air of calm urgency.

Let's hurry. Form the gateway and let the wrap judge our worth.

The Astryn's now move into position, spreading out in precise formation, their triangular faces glowing brighter as they channel their combined essence. Waves of light ripple outward merging with the prismatic arcs of the rainbow falls above them. The air becomes dense with energy, vibrating the harmonious interplay of light and sound.

Each Astryn's light pulses with its unique hue. Lunaara stands at the center; her grey glow intensifies as she begins to weave their combined energies into a cohesive force. The musical lands below them resonate in harmony, each note amplifying with the Astryn's efforts. As their lights converge, a vortex begins to form-a swirling column of luminescent energy rising into the heavens. The vortex pulses with a rhythm akin to a heartbeat, each thrum sending ripples through the fabric of space itself.

Lunaara's glow deepens further, her essence expanding outward to stabilize the structure. Her light shifts in intricate patterns, each hue blending seamlessly into the vortex's rhythm.

Indigo streaks blend into emerald waves of balance and strength across its body forming intricate patterns of circles.

This bridge will carry us to the Wrap but its stability demands unity; the slightest disruption will shatter it and leave us in the void.

As the gateway nears completion one Astryn floats closer-Its form now lit with crimson, its glow flickering with tension.

Deep red flares into jagged bursts of orange.

Are we certain this will hold? The wrap is no ordinary place it will reject us entirely.

In response to this comes another Astryn countering the first one by radiating

Soft spirals of blue edged with radiant silver steaks.

Doubt is our greatest enemy. Trust the bridge.

The gateway now begins to solidify; it's light surging in brilliance as the Astryn's and Lunaara prepare to enter it. But just as they align themselves for the crossing Lunaara's light flickers faintly, a disturbance rippling through the vortex.

A swirl of deep indigo fractures into jagged yellow leading to streaks of red.

There is an imbalance, a shadow among us. The wrap will not forgive treachery.

Her warnings hang heavy in the air as the gateway pulses ominously, its light intensifying as though sensing the unspoken discord.

The gateway surges, its spiraling light twisting with an almost sentient pulse, reacting to the energies feeding into it. The tension among the Astryns and Lunaara is palpable. The glowing forms of the Astryns began casting long, fragmented shadows across the iridescent ground. Lunaara grey essence trembles faintly her powers stretched thin as she anchors the bridge.

One of the Astryns now moves closer its body radiating no light at all without warning shoots concentrated beams of harpoon shaped lightning bolts slicing through the blue lit Astryn's glow its light now flickering violently, its form beginning to dim but not fade away.

The third Astryn now floats in front of the traitor Astryn.

Radiating violent golden lights that erupt into jagged, fractured bursts of pinkish orange forming random patterns which make no sense.

What have you done? And why?

The wounded Astryn now radiates its body in

Dim blue and fractured patters of what looks to be semi triangles.

Betrayal! You, you have turned against us but why?

The traitor Astryn now bright up its light tinged with streaks of shadowy black, and it lunges forward for another attack unleashing jet-black an array of jet black light bolts. In response to this the third Astryn now begins to shoot array light bolts of assorted colors. This blast of light and dark now collides causing shockwaves through the universe. The land beneath them now begins to tremble, the musical tones turning discordant, echoing the chaos.

Lunaara now steps forward and radiates its body in

Violet fractures which lead to jagged streaks of yellow and red making the shape of U.

Stop! The bridge will collapse if this continues.

To which the traitor Astryn responds by radiating its body in

Zig Zag lines of red which gradually turn into straight lines of whites.

Exactly my plan.

The third Astryn then radiates its body by

Forming random patterns of Orange which makes no sense.

But why?

To which finally the traitor Astryn responds by

Forming spirals of Dark red jagged into sharp black and orange patterns of malevolence leading to curved lines of jet black.

Drakaara's will is too much to challenge. You all really think you can challenge Drakaara? That you can challenge Darkness itself? I have understood the truth of this universe. Light is blinding but darkness is liberating. It was me who turned you both against Lunaara right at its birth because I could sense its purpose. I tried warning you at every step but seem you all are fond of action. I have made a deal with Drakaara. A deal to serve her.

This revelation strikes like a thunderclap, sending ripples of continuous shockwave across the universe. So the third Astryn now forms a cosmic sword made from purely silver light and hurls it on to the traitor Astryn. However the traitor Astryn completely blocks the attack using a cosmic translucent shield made of eerie jet black glittering lights.

The two Astryn's clash their beams of light and dark colliding in mid air, creating bursts of a contrast of light and dark, sparkles of which are also scattered across and inside the vortex leading to the gateway now trembling under the strain, its once stable spiral now wobbling precariously. Lunaara pushes her power to the lither grey glow deepening into a fierce protective aura. Both(The injured and the Third Astryn) radiate their bodies

In golden lights interfaced with streaks of urgent green making patterns of straight extremely speed pulsating lights.

Lunaara take the bridge! Leave us behind if you must, the wrap cannot fall to Drakaara.

And that is when entire the rainbow falls suddenly come to a halt, the otherwise pink skies of Ology now begin to turn golden, the lands now begin to regain its composure and music. The continuous shockwaves now come to a halt, and the treacherous Astryn's body now starts radiating with random lights and patterns. The other 2 Astryns and Lunaara now bow at the arrival of their savior. At the arrival of Eldarion.

Chapter 12: The Divine Intervention

The skies of Ology shuddered as if recoiling from the force that now tore through its ethereal beauty. A golden rift opened in its pink skies. This was no ordinary arrival for this was Eldarion descending onto the musical lands of Ology with a presence that demanded submission of reality itself.

He descended slowly, his form now radiating with a unique combination of serenity and rage. Threads of pure light and shadow wove its body, shifting like living armor. His triangular face shone with an unsettling perfection, crystalline yet darker than the void between the stars. The inverted trees whose floating once swayed with the delicate rhythm of Kolog's beauty froze mid motion as if held in awe- or dread.

The scent of his arrival was not thunder, but a deep resonance that spread through Ology. Silencing even its rainbow falls. The droplets that usually fell like shimmering prisms dimmed in his presence, their vibrant hues muted under the weight of his gaze. Beneath his feet, the magical lands resonated with his energy.

Eldarion's eyes twin suns of unyielding gold, surveyed the land with an intensity that pierced even the translucent forms of Astryn. The planet itself seemed to hold its breath. His arrival was not plain but a proclamation of Judgment, a herald of reckoning.

With a single gesture Eldarion raised his hand and the air itself seemed to bend. Charged with an unseen energy. The traitor Astryn usually radiant with its shifting light patterns now dimmed in fear. Its form began flickering in fear beyond measure and then silence.

Ology waited trembling under the weight of Eldarion's wraith as the moment stretched into eternity.

The silence was now suffocating. The Astryn's stood motionless their usual patterns of light muted to dull shifting shades of red and maroon indicating fear and uncertainty. Eldarion's golden gaze fell upon the quivering Astryn, his presence intensifying with a crushing weight that made the air itself hum with tension. The musical lands beneath him cracked slightly, their harmony disrupted by the vibrations of Eldarion's anger.

The Astryns translucent forms now began to radiate in random patterns of whites and Silvers. It was a collective question.

Asking what punishment would Eldarion bring.

Their lights made subtle, barely perceptible shifts of intensity and hue, yet they conveyed volumes of emotion: Reverence, Fear and Morbid Curiosity.

Eladarion's form remained still, his triangular face casting sharp crystalline shadows as he raised his hand to silence their flickering patterns. A beam of Gold light thin but piercing shot from his palm and engulfed the guilty Astryn. **His body now began radiating in Thick gold and silver lines making patterns of erratic shapes unknown to the universe but understood by the Astryn's.**

Therion- You have betrayed us.

The other Astryn dimmed their glow while the injured Astryn glow was constantly dimming with each passing moment. The other Astryn along with the injured Astryn distanced themselves from Therion.

The other Astryn's body now pulsating with brief patterns of mourning: Soft blues spiraling into tiny crescents.

A symbolic expression for sorrow of the betrayal.

Therion's erratic patterns grew frantic, his light stuttering between pale greens and sharp purples.

A desperate plea for mercy.

Eldarion's response was swift and merciless. His form darkened in golden light fading into an ominous crimson making patterns of blizzards that pulsed like a heartbeat of a star on the verge of collapse.

You dare use our sacred patterns to lie? To plead for forgiveness when you guilt is etched into the very fabric of your being?

Eldarion floated forward, his towering form radiating an intensity that seemed to distort the space around him.

Eldarion's now projected its light outwards tearing through the air like a storm. The skies above mirrored his wrath, streaked with violent hues of red and black. His hand rose, light twisting and coalescing into an intricate pattern that radiated outward.- A web of Golden and crimson tendrils that ensnared dances, carrying a message not just for Therion but for all the Astryns and Lunaara.

Betrayal should be met with annihilation.

Therion's form now began to crack under the weight of Eldarion's wrath.

His desperate lights shifted again this time into a series of fragmented lines and erratic bursts.

Conveying regret but the patterns dissolved almost as quickly as they formed, his guilt and fear breaking the ability to communicate.

Eladrion's body now pulsated with fractured bursts of dark gold, red and Black forming intricate patterns of constellations and stars.

You fractured the sanctity of being an Astryn. You allowed the secrets of light to spill beyond the veil. It was you who informed Drakaara of the Cosmic Wrap.

Your betrayal is not merely a crime against us- It's an affront to light itself.

Eldarion unleashed a final, blinding pattern-An array of pulsating beams that formed a perfect a weapon. A weapon never seen before by the Astryn's. It was a wheel. A wheel born of celestial light and forged by the lights of Eldarion form. This was no ordinary wheel for it was a radiant halo of the cosmos. A blazing sun caught in eternal motion. It was surrounded by blades, each blade whispers the hymns of creation and destruction. In its center is a void, the silent eye of eternity. While its edges made of light slicing though darkness and betrayal. When summoned it tears through the air with a thunderous roar.

Therion let out its final lights outwards. These lights had all the colors of the rainbow as the blade shattered its diamond body into shards of broken glass.

Eldarion now looked at the injured Astryn and let out warm but relaxing bursts of gold and silver ultrasound waves healing it totally.

The diamond forms of both the Astryn's and Lunaara now pulsated in bright green and bright yellow forming perfect triangles.

A symbolic of collective gratitude and relief.

Eldarion now turned to Lunaara and the other Astryn's his radiant form once more commanding mix of light and pattern.

His body now pulsating with solid bright gold, green blue and white making patterns of calming waves.

Order has been restored, but balance remains fragile. Let no one test my wrath again.

And with that the skies of Ology trembled once last time before turning pink again as though the planet itself had its breath in the wake of Eldarion's fury for this was the return of Eldarion to Junkin.

As Therion's soul was dragged into the void, the world around him dissolved into a smothering darkness. He fell through endless nothingness, the fabric of existence unraveling around him, stripping away every connection every sense of safety. The soothing hum of Kolog's lands was gone, replaced by a deafening silence that seemed to devour sound itself.

When he finally landed it was not upon solid ground, but a shifting shadowy expanse. The surface beneath him writhed like a living thing, cold and unyielding, yet moving as if to swallow him whole. The void began to shift, shadows pooling and coalescing into grotesque shapes.

Then came the voices.

They were not sounds but echoes- Vibrations of his deepest regrets and darkest fears, twisting into an unnatural symphony. The whispers were accusatory, rising and falling into chaotic waves. He has betrayed the Astryn's, Lunaara and Eladrion. He was unworthy of light.

The darkness began to take form from the void emerged twisted spectral figures-Demons born of Therion's guilt. They were not foreign entities, but grotesque reflection of himself, their translucent shapes twisted into monstrous parodies of his own light. Their faces were jagged their bodies fragmented and their movements erratic, as if they struggled to contain the weight of their own existence.

The largest demon loomed over Therion, its body pulsated with a slickly green that mirrored his movements of cowardice forming erratic bursts of silver, grey and indigo forming images of Astrtyn's, Lunaara and Eladrion.

Why did you do it Therion? Why did you betray the Astryn's, Lunaara and Eldarion?

Therion stepped back, his patterns faltering into desperate bursts of white and blue.

A pitiful attempt at denial, but the demons laughed, their mocking voices reverberating through the void.

The demon's body now began to pulsate in bursts of Crimson, Red and Black forming patterns "X" leading to images of Skulls.

Denial won't save you here. Your guilt is the architect of your torment.

His jagged form shifting closer. Around him, the other demons began to close in. Each one bore the colors and patterns of his darkest memories: The red streaks of anger when he first entertained betrayal, the violet pulses of fear when he made his choice, and the black voids of despair that consumed him after the act.

They attacked not with physical blows, but with the weight of his own emotions. The largest demon raised a clawed hand and slashed through Therion's light, shattering it further. The pain was unbearable not from the wound itself, but from the flood of memories it unleashed images of the Astryn's he had betrayed, of Lunaara he had betrayed, Of Eldarion he has betrayed, their trusting light fading into the shadows as his treachery fostered their hunger.

Therion tried to feel his light flickering weakly as he stumbled through the endless expanse. But the ground shifted beneath him, reshaping itself to drag him back towards the demons.

The demon's body now pulsated in Grey to silver to jet black lights forming patterns of jagged, fractured spirals of Fibonacci.

You cannot escape this hell. You will live this torment over and over again.

The void around them shifted again, and the shadowy expanse gave way for a twisted recreation of Ology. But this was no longer the serene, magical world he had once known. The skies were blood-red, the rainbow falls pouring rivers of black ichors. The musical lands groaned with discordant, haunting notes that scraped against his mind.

The demons dragged him to the center of the nightmare, forcing him to watch as fractured, ghostly versions of the Astryn's he had betrayed emerged from the shadows.

Therion's light flickered one last time before dimming almost to nothingness. He sank to his knees, his form trembling as the full weight of his guilt bore down upon him and still the demon circled their forms shifting and multiplying feeding off his anguish. In the distance, the void shimmered faintly, hinting at the escape that would never come. Therion was trapped, his punishment not of fire or brimstone, but of his own making a relentless, inescapable hell where his guilt would haunt him for all eternity.

Chapter 13: Shadow Pole

In the vast expanse of the cosmos there lay no greater terror than the **SHADOW POLE.** It is not just an artifact- It is a harbinger of annihilation, a weapon crafted to erase the slightest ray of light from existence. Forged from the energy of three of the brightest of the stars in the universe. It was no ordinary staff, it stood tall and foreboding, wrapped in Jet Black Obsidian, Its surface flittering faintly like shattered stars trapped in the void. Yet unlike the comforting shimmer of celestial light, its glitter was cold, sharp and unsettling. Continuous rhythmic flashes erupted from it like ice cold blizzards. It looked like a predator's eyes moments before it strikes.

The shadow pole was a thing of elegance. It form was long and smooth, yet its body rippled with unnatural curves as though it is molded by the very hands of the creator itself. The surface was adorned with dark veins, moving in patterns that shift with each passing moment, never settling, always restless.

At the top of the staff, a core pulsed with a terrifying black orb. The orb is the staff's heart, and it seemed to suck in the very light that dared to touch it. It did not glow with the warm, inviting hues of a star but instead, it emitted an eerie, sickly black light. This faint glow was not illuminating; it was absorbing, bending everything around it into a hollow, impenetrable void. It was as though the orb itself is a black hole- A force with the power to consume not only the light but also the very essence of life itself.

The pole's presence is more than oppressive-It is suffocating. It seemed to distort the fabric of the universe itself, warping reality in subtle but profound ways. When it is close the stars above flickered and dimmed, their light trembling as if in fear. Even the deepest corners of the cosmos recoiled from its sinister energy. To be in the Shadow Pole's proximity is to feel light, life creation itself shudder. As if the very flow of existence is held in suspension, uncertain and trembling at the brink of collapse.

Its creation is a mystery one that no scholar had ever fully unraveled. Some believe it had been forged in the final moments of a dying star, its power born from death theories of a celestial giant. Others speculated that it had been Birthed on the cold, dark void between the stars where not even light could escape. Legends told of an ancient, nameless being that had shaped the staff, using the raw material of the void itself to create an object of pure destruction. No one knew for sure but they all agreed on one thing. The Shadow Pole is a weapon unlike any other.

The staff's core thrummed with energy older than the universe itself, a primal force. Its black glow does not merely illuminate, it devours. Where it passed, it left only emptiness behind. Light was bent, devoured and swallowed into its core, leaving a haunting nothingness in its wake. The very air around it is heavy with the weight of its presence as if the universe itself is being drained of its vibrancy, replacing a suffocating gloom that clings to everything it touches.

The shadow pole is not merely a staff but a symbol of defiance against creation itself. Drakaara understood its significance. For millenniums she has searched the stars, galaxies, constellations her obsession growing with each passing millennium. To her light is an illusion. An illusion that robs nature of its true self. Of its true darkness. She saw Shadow Pole as the only chance of returning nature to its true form. With this artifact in hand she will finally be able to pierce the cosmic wrap, the fragile tapestry that held the universe in balance. The Shadow Pole once pierced in the Cosmic Wrap would return nature back to its true self, drained of light , life and magic.

The pole has a strange resonance as if it recognized its destined wielder. When Drakaara finally combined the energy, life and light of Crystallium, Emrithar and Pulsitar to form the Shadow Pole. She feels a strange connection to it. The Shadow Pole is reacting to her touch. The glittering obsidian seemed to come alive under her grip. It is no longer a relic but a tool of unfathomable power. She could feel its strength coursing through her, its dark energy amplifying her very strength of her own.

The shadow pole was cold-Colder than anything Drakaara had ever known. Colder than Drakaara herself. Its touch felt like death itself, its chill seeping into her very darkness. The material hard and unyielding begins to drain the warmth of thee air. The orb at its peak is throbbing with a power that made the stars themselves tremble. Shadow Pole began to boost Drakaara's darkness. Her darkness is now beginning to elevate to absolute dark. Allowing Drakaara to not just manipulate laws of the dark but also laws of light, creation and nature itself. With it she could now. The black orb at its core was the key. The gateway to the powers of absolute dark. In her mind Drakaara could already hear the whispers of the staff. They are promises. Promises of power beyond imagination. The more she listens, the more clearer the promises became. The Shadow Pole was not merely a weapon it was the end of all light, life and creation. The ultimate expression of destruction. She was feeling the pull of the pole, urging her to act, to pierce it in the Cosmic Wrap. And Drakaara with her mission to return nature back to its original true form, its true darkness now with the power of absolute dark was finally ready.

With the Shadow Pole she would fulfill her purpose, her mission. She is now ready to rewrite history, the fate of the cosmos and no one-nothing will stand in her way. The stars will fade, galaxies would cripple, universes would collapse and darkness itself will bow to her will. The end has come and with it the birth of a new orders where only darkness will reign.

Drakaara still floating on the now lifeless husk of Pulsitar, gazed into the vastness of the cosmos. She had already accomplished half of her mission by capturing the life, light and energies of 3 of the brightest stars of the universe and forging them to form the Shadow Pole. Now she just needed to find the final key the Cosmic Wrap.

And to locate the co-ordinates of the Cosmic Wrap Drakaara would need to perform a ritual, one that would pull the very threads of reality. This was no simple divination or star gazing. The cosmic wrap was after all the cradle of existence, the nexus of light. Only the most arcane and forbidden magic could pierce through the dark folds of existence and reveal its hidden location in the Kaelyon Constellation.

With a deep measure breath, Drakaara began. She extended her arms, pulling the dust from the air the dead remnants of the frozen, lifeless particles of the stars and planets previously captured in her paintings gathered in a swirling mass before her. Each fragment seemed to pulse with an eerie light of its own. The energy of countless lost planets and stars now serving a single purpose.

She raised her hands high and the dust began to spin in a spiraling vortex. The dead planets and star's energies surged and hummed, almost alive with the echoes of their once glorious existence. She summoned their energies through a deep, wordless thought while casting a spell on each of these energies.

The dust twisted and formed into patterns, each moving to the beat of a rhythm only Drakaara understood. She began to weave these energies into a magical glowing dark dust creating a spiral of absolute dark energy. As the dust touched these long lost planets and stars they seemed to shudder as if waking from a deep slumber. Their surfaces now crackled emitting a ghostly glow. As they absorbed the energy of the dead worlds around them.

With her will focused, Drakaara sent these energies into every direction of the vast emptiness of the space, sending them out like boomerangs of forgotten light and energy in search of the co-ordinates she needed. The only way to locate the Kaelyon Constellation.

The frozen lifeless particles of planets and stars locked in a spell moved through space in a trance but this time with an eerie glow flashing against the void like cold, dead lanterns. Each of them bound to return like echoes lost in the endless night. As they moved they left a trail of shimmering star skulls, a path only visible to Drakaara.

The ritual was complete. The dead planet and stars have guided her.

Drakaara could feel it now, the Shadow Pole began to vibrate lightly in her hands. The Kaelyon Constellation is no longer hidden from her, its position is clear etched into the fabric of the universe itself. The dead lanterns now carrying the map of the cosmos' deepest secrets began to return back inside her dark canvas. One by one they come back guiding her to her ultimate prize- The Cosmic Wrap.

With a final breath, Drakaara opened her eyes, her hands still trembling with the vibrations from the Shadow Pole. She could see it now-The co-ordinates of the Kaelyon Constellation shining bright within her, ready to lead her to the Wrap's hiding place.

Chapter 14: Moments of Doom

Drakaara now ready to server her purpose, began to float carefully on the shimmering trails ahead of her. The air around her was thick with the weight of the silence, pressing in from all sides. She was no longer in any realm she had known- This was an abyss, a vastness where the very idea of space seemed to disintegrate. The path ahead was a faint shimmer, delicate and ethereal, yet impossibly precise. Like the final breath of the dying cosmos.

The trail twisted and spiraled undulating with a strange, glowing pulse. It wasn't a physical path-more like a ripple. Each movement Drakaara made was mirrored by the shimmering trail beneath her feet, drawing her deeper into the unknown. As she moved forward, the shadows around her deepened, stretching and bending in unnatural ways. As if the universe has forgotten the rules of its own creation.

Drakaara's senses heightened every sound muffled by the sheer emptiness around her. The remnants of ancient crumbling stars and planets drifted by fragments of celestial bodies long captured in her paintings now. She passed them with a quiet reverence knowing that their death was the precursor to a new beginning.

Her heart beat in excitement as she pressed onwards the glowing trail guiding her like a tether to the cosmic wrap. The farther she travelled the more she felt an overwhelming force pulling at her from the depths ahead. A ripple almost imperceptible fitted through the void. Then another. A wave of bright white light energy washed over her face thick slowing down her movements. She knew from the eons of wisdom that this light wave was emerging from the core of the cosmic wrap, cosmic wrap served as the nexus of light.

The path beneath her shifted in sudden bursts of chaotic light, flickering like embers, But Drakaara did not falter for she knew that this was no ordinary journey. This was a passage- A scared crossing which is leading her to the heart of the universe itself and every step she took carried her closer to it all.

With each passing step the energy of the void seemed to collapse in on itself, pressing in with an almost suffocating pressure yet Drakaara felt no fear. Her resolve was absolute, her purpose unyielding. She had crossed the threshold of her destiny.

Ahead the darkness and light seemed to churn, swirling in patterns that were both beautiful and terrifying. This was the point of no return. The Cosmic Wrap- the nexus of all existence loomed ahead- A place where creation and destruction collided, a place where everything she had ever known would dissolve and be reborn and she would be the one to re shape it all.

As she stepped on the final trail the air thickened around her and the once steady shimmer of the Cosmic Wrap before her now flickered erratically as it were being obscured by a shifting veil of primordial magic. The darkness around her deepened, the void pressing in her like a suffocating blanket. Her senses were assaulted by the weight of the ancient forces that had been dormant for millennia. The place was not meant to be entered by anyone. But Drakaara felt even closer to her purpose. So she pressed forward, knowing that the entrance of the Cosmic Wrap is protected but what she was not aware that it would let her pass without trials.

As she advanced the air began to hum vibrating with an energy she had never felt before- An energy that reverberated through her very bones. It felt like the heartbeat of the universe itself, the rhythm of life and death entwined. And then, without warning the first test emerged.

The ground beneath her feet trembled and the space around her twisted into impossible shapes. A massive rift tore through the sky and from it emerged a swirling vortex of Shadow and Light, its edges crackling with raw chaotic magic. It sought to tear her apart.

Drakaara did not flinch, she had prepared for this moment and with a snap of her fingers, a dark snake shaped creature shout out followed by a long dark tendrils wrapping around the rift. The vortex recoiled but it was relentless thrashing against her power. The rift was a manifestation of a primordial force that held the universe's balance and it was sentient aware of her intent to breach its sanctum.

For a moment the rift pulsed with an ancient intelligence, its currents of energy swirling around her, trying to disorient and paralyze her with fear. But Drakaara knew no fear she drew from the deepest recesses of her power- The power that had been cultivated through years of capturing light, life and energies from galaxies, stars and planets, with a scream that vibrated through the air she now shot thick waves of absolute darkness from her eyes while forcing her dark tendrils into the rift using her own essence to bind it. The rift writhed violently, but eventually, it succumbed to her will, with a final snap the vortex imploded in on itself, dissipating into nothingness from which it had emerged.

Breathing heavily, Drakaara took another step, her body trembling from exertion, but her spirit unwavering for she knew this was just the beginning. As she advanced deeper into the void, the temperature plummeted. The very air became thick with the chill of death and the shadows grew heavier, pulling at her from all directions. It was as if the universe itself was trying to freeze her in place, to trap her within its icy grip. But Drakaara would not be imprisoned. Her heart pulsed with darkness itself and the cold was nothing as compared to her blood. But then a new challenge arose. The very ground beneath her feet cracked open, revealing a bottomless chasm that stretched out into an endless void, it was a test of perception designed to break her resolve. She knew it in her heart one step closer and she would be lost, one step backwards and she will never be able to leave .She had to choose wisely for this is the test of fate.

Drakaara looked into the chasm, her breath steady, and her mind clear. She could feel the weight of the test trying to worm its way into her thoughts but she would not succumb. With a slow, deliberate movement, she extended her hand over the chasm, her fingers grazing the edge. The darkness responded, the void shifting and pulsing with its own sentence. It was testing her will, her strength of purpose.

Without hesitation, Drakaara stepped forward. Letting the darkness consume her for a brief moment before she re asserted her control over darkness and her senses. The chasm collapsed inwards and the path before her cleared once more. She knew now the trials were just about her power-They were test of her inner strength, her resolve to see the mission through to the end.

She continues on and as the void around her shifted an oppressive silence descended. For a moment the darkness was no complete that she felt home.

But then from the depths of the silence shadows twisted, taking on monstrous forms that flickered in and out of existence, their twisted shapes lurching towards her. Their movements were erratic, disjointed and unnatural. This was no ordinary physical foe: It was a test of the mind. The shadows seemed to reach into her consciousness attempting to plant doubts, to unravel her resolve.

For the first time in this journey, Drakaara felt the weight of her purpose. Her mind swirled with the impossible visions of what might happen if she failed. She steadied herself, drawing deep from her well of darkness and power. She screamed as the force of her necromantic energy pressed upon them. She sent waves of her power crashing through them, banishing the illusions one by one.

With that, the final barrier fell. The cosmic wrap lay ahead, shrouded in a veil of impenetrable darkness, but now Drakaara was ready. The tests have been oncoming and she would not fail. She now stood at the threshold of the Cosmic Wrap. The void around her seemed to bend and ripple stretching into an infinite blackness that consumed everything. It was singularity that contained within it the life force and magic of the universe itself. It pulsed gently rhythmically as if breathing in the air of creation.

The final test had been brutal, but Drakaara was unwavering. Her body was battered, her mind exhausted, yet her resolve was a forge of steel. There was no turning back. She had come too far, crossed too many thresholds, fought too many battles. She will not stop now.

The shadow pole in her hand hummed, its dark power thrumming like a living entity, ready to fulfill its purpose. As she stepped into the Cosmic Wrap, the air thickened, the darkness coiling around her like a serpent. She could feel the immense force that held this place together-The source of all creation, all life, and all magic. But here in the heart of it, was also the potential for utter destruction.

Her steps echoed in the void, a sound that reverberated through the infinite blackness, disturbing the stillness that had long ruled this place. Slowly, she approached the center of the Cosmic Wrap. It was like stepping into the eye of an ancient storm, a silent center where all things converged.

Drakaara raised the Shadow Pole. Feeling its energy surge within her. The dark magic within it responded to the cosmic presence, feeding off the very essence of this place. The pole thrummed as if in anticipation. Her fingers wrapped around the pole tightly, the grip of fate itself.

She had arrived.

With a violent, wrenching motion. Drakaara plunged the Shadow Pole into the Cosmic Wrap. The moment the pole touched the core of this ancient, unyielding power, the entire universe seemed to tremble. A shockwave of dark energy exploded outwards rippling the through the universe. The Cosmic Wrap screamed, an unbearable guttural wail that echoed through the realms as if the universe itself was being torn apart.

The dark energy around Drakaara thickened into a tangible substance; Swirling, swirling and pulsating as if alive. The shadow pole began to glow with an unnatural, inky light as it merged with the very essence of the universe.

The moment the Shadow Pole embedded fully into the womb of the Cosmic Wrap, the ground beneath Drakaara's feet shattered giving way to an overwhelming torrent of energy. It felt like the very core of the universe was being drawn into the pole, as though it had become a reverse conduit of every realm, every spark of life, and every flame of creation. The pole' dark light began to suck every light, every creation, every planet, every constellation, and every star in its wake. Life itself seemed to wilt, the pulse of existence had been picked from the threads of reality. Stars flickered, their light dimming as if their powers were being siphoned away into Shadow Pole. The ground under Drakaara's feet crumbled and she floated, suspended in the center of the Cosmic Wrap. Her heart raced, her breath shallow, but her mind was calm, she could feel the energy of the universe being siphoned into the pole and with every breath, the balance of existence was tipping further into the chaos.

Around her, the stars blinked out one by one, consumed by the ravenous maw of the Shadow Pole. The light of the moon faded, leaving nothing but an eternal night even the very essence of magic, the force that had shaped the worlds, began to fray and unravels. The very pulse of creation had slowed. Becoming weaker and the universe groaned beneath the strain of losing itself.

Drakaara now touched the Shadow Pole, feeling the power coursing through her veins, consuming her own essence along with the rest of the universe. But this was her purpose, her destiny. The universe is now finally returning to its true form. Back to eternal darkness.

As the Shadow Pole activated fully, the ripples it caused spread far beyond the Cosmic Wrap. The entire cosmos seemed to shudder as the first of the universal lights began to extinguish. Realms began to bleed into one another, as the source of magic and life were pulled away from their origins drawn to the insatiable hunger of the Shadow Pole.

Across the universe civilizations were gripped by a sudden, inexplicable darkness. The starts above their worlds dimmed and the lifeblood of the universe- Its light, its energy, it's very creation- Began to vanish. Those who had once wielded magic found their powers fading, their spells weakening as the wellspring of energy drained away. The pull of the Shadow Pole was not just a drain- It was a curse, an insidious hunger that devoured everything in its wake.

Drakaara felt the weight of this destruction, and she embraced it. The shadows surrounded her, pulling tighter, twisting around her body as she became the vessel for this dark transformation. The destruction was beautiful in her own twisted way, an art of annihilation and in the heart of it all stood Drakaara.

Chapter 15: Retaliation

The Astryn's once unshakable, calm shattered as their diamond like bodies begin to pulse erratically glowing in frantic bursts of light. The air around them thickened with tension, the sharp, jagged rays of their forms slicing through the otherwise serine landscape of Ology. It was as though the universe itself had lost its harmony vibrating with a dissonance only they could feel. Each Astryn's body flickered with an unnatural intensity as their once –smooth crystalline surfaces cracked, revealing deep blue veins of energy that pulsed with urgency. The echoes of this disturbance reverberated through the fabric of the universe itself.

The sky above them, an untouched canvas of soft pink and muted purples, now seemed to waver, flickering in strange shades of green and red. Kolog's usual tranquil atmosphere now began to quake in resonance with the new disturbance shifting within Ology and the Astryn's-This was an anomaly, an unnatural disturbance and they could feel it coursing through them. The Shadow Pole was extending its reach far beyond the farthest reaches of the universe.

The first Astryn's diamond body now began to glow in a chaotic blend of Blue and Violet, titled their head upward, its glow stuttered like a dying star.

It's happening, the shadow Pole is absorbing everything, the stars, the planets, the constellations, every creation, every light, and Ology is next.

The second Astryn its form more refined in its gentle swirls of pale green and soft gold, shifted uneasily through its body trying to form broken patterns of circles but in vain.

The pull… it is so powerful now we cannot stop it our energy, Kolog's energy is draining, our energy is draining, All light, life and energy from the universe is draining we need to act quick.

When a crackle of dark energy tore through the air, sending tremors through Kolog's very bones. The Astryn's bodies stilled for a moment, the glow in their diamond forms growing softer as they sought to process the weight of this revelation.

But Lunaara- her calm presence an unwavering beacon of calm was already preparing. Her form began to gleam with sharp patterns of circle, triangle and pentagons in lights of bright Red, Crimson and Maroon.

We must act now, the Cosmic Wrap, it is our only hope to stop the Shadow Pole from devouring the universe.

The first Astryn's body now began to form jagged, broken patterns of random strings leading to finally form a spider web which then splits into sets of tiny dots resembling the stars in lights of yellow, orange and Red.

But Lunaara the cosmic wrap is a myth no creature in existence has ever seen it and even if it does exist how can we find it?

The second Astryn's body now began to broken patterns of tiny, cloud like structures in lights of bright gold and green.

Puffin! If anyone can guide us, it is him.

Learning this Lunaara exchanged uneasy glances with the Astryn's not knowing who Puffin is, not sure if Puffin can be trusted especially after the earlier reveal about the spy Astryn. But with no other option left they set aside their paranoia, fear. The Astryn's bodies now began to pulse in synchronized patterns, their light bending and coiling as they prepared to summon Puffin, the energy in the air now began to vibrate with new energy.

The Astryns stood in a tense silence, their diamond-like bodies flickered erratically almost ghastly with bright anxious bursts of light. The dissonance in their movements was mirrored in their lights which they now projected outwards which clashed like stars collapsing into themselves. They had always prided themselves on their unshakable unity but now with the universe on the brink of destruction, cracks were appearing. One of them pulsed with sharp hues of gold and red while the other flickered with an agitated mix of green and purple. Their inner conflict was manifesting in chaotic patterns of light that swirled violently around them. Their combined energies and lights sent out a fury of white and blue sparkles. Their bodies contracted, the shimmering lights around them flickering like lightning on a stormy night.

Together the two Astryn's synchronized their energies, their lights entwining and shifting in intricate patterns that began to form a portal in the space between them. Their combined effort pulsed like a living entity, the light bending and curving in graceful arcs, forming like a shimmering gateway that cracked open the very fabric of reality.

As the portal stabilized, the air around them crackled with an electric charge, a deep rumbling vibration filling the atmosphere. As the portal reached its peak they felt it-A surge of chaotic, boundless energy. With one final burst they opened the gate completely summoning Puffin into Kolog.

The moment the portal opened, a burst of light and sound surged from it- Electric bolts of blue and purple crackled through the air like a thunderstorm unleashed right into Kolog. The vibrant energy hummed with the promise of chaos.

And it finally happened. With a burst of gleaming light Puffin appeared.

He arrived in a whirl of colors-The blues, the pinks, the yellows, and the greens, blending together in a riotous symphony of hues. The space around him trembled with a low rumble and in an instant, the atmosphere shifted. Where once they had been clam, now the air was alive with the sounds of crackling thunder and the blinding flashes of lightening. As if the very sky was laughing and trembling together.

Puffin bought along him a relief of playful energy. He was a three ounce cloud. Just like the other clouds he could shift his shape. His entire energy was like a kaleidoscope of brightness. His body rippled with a constant movement like an abstract sculpture in motion-Puffin had a knack for pranks. His eyes always gleamed with mischief. His smile made of bright orbs of light.

He spun around the air softly- His voice soft but thunderous it was not scary but an underlying playful melody that made the very air vibrate.

His body threw out dancing, vibrating rays of bright yellow and orange light, followed by a loud crack of thunder.

Missing me already? Huh?

But the Astryn's were still tensed, they exchanged wary glances. Their bodies glowing with unease.

The first Astryn pulses with a mix of bright gold, orange and red forming sharp flickers of human like arms through its body but made of nebulas.

No time for jokes Puffin. Drakaara has initiated the purge of the universe.

The second Astryn too now pulsated with jagged, sharp and erratic lights of pink, violet and red thereby forming patterns of fireflies' random constellations.

Puffin we need your help to find Kaelyon constellation.

But Puffin seemed to unfazed by their worries. Instead he twirled midair, sending out sparks of light and waves as thunder as he danced around them now smiling, his movements erratic and unpredictable.

I see, your tension my light friends but a lit fun has never harmed anyone. Has it?

Lunaara standing off the side, took a step forward, her eyes narrowing. She had been observing Puffin with suspicion from the start, unable to shake the feeling that the creature's chaotic nature might be a little too dangerous. Her heart beat faster yet she was drawn to the exuberance Puffin exuded.

She now pulsated broken, lights of soft blue, pink, purple forming question marks made of stars through its body however these lights were continuously vibrating.

Do you know where it is? The cosmic wrap?

At her lights, Puffin stopped mid-spin and turned toward her with a wild grin. And started realizing bolts of thunder in the forms of circles resembling tornadoes.

You are a clever one, aren't you? Straight to the point. But everything has a price my dear. You need to earn the co-ordinates.

Lunaara now began pulsating in mixes of Yellow, orange and pink making patterns of star shaped question marks through her body.

Earn them? How?

Puffin winked and twirled anticlockwise spitting out short bolts of thunder and bright white lights from his mouth.

A game of light and thunder. Catch me and the co-ordinate are yours.

And with that Puffin darted away in a flash of lightning, his form blurring with joy and excitement as the air around them vibrated with the sound thunder.

Lunaara stood still for a moment, her heart pounding as the lightning flashed across the sky and Puffin darted away in a blur of color. His laughter echoed around her, rippling through the air like a playful breeze. The sudden intensity of chaotic energy sent a chill down her spine, but it also awakened something within her-A spark of excitement, of challenge. This was something she had never felt before.

With a sudden movement she took forward, the ground beneath her feet humming with the energy of Kolog. The air shimmered with soft waves of Pink and purple light and the inverted trees now began dancing as if responding to the sudden shift in the atmosphere.

Puffin was quick, his form now a whirl of brightness and color zipping through the air with ease. He now released soft lights of blues and violets only to tease Lunaara.

Faster, Faster.

Lunaara now clenched her firsts, her gaze now narrowing as she focused on the light patterns in the sky. He was fast but so was she. She had trained, she had honed her powers and now she would prove it.

So she closed her eyes for a fraction of a second and when she opened them again, the world around her seemed to slow. Her light patterns shifted with precision, each pulse a deliberate step in a dance. She stretched her arms wide, weaving her fingers through the air as soft lines of violet and gold spiraled outward cutting through the vastness of the sky like ribbons. Her body responded , light and agile as she moved with swift, controlled grace mirroring the patterns she created.

Puffin however was not as easily caught. He zipped through the air in unpredictable directions, sending blasts of electric blue and white lightning shooting out in all directions. His laughter rang through the air, louder and more jubilant than ever.

The energy around them crackled with this playful challenge and Lunaara's frustration began to grow. She had always been the one to control. But Puffin was chaos incarnate and his every move was an invitation to play.

She took another step forward, her footfall light yet purposeful. She was close now-Closer than she had been before. Puffin in his endless spiral of colors, seemed to be enjoying the chase, flashing in and out of view with every burst of thunder. The air hummed with his energy, but Lunaara was undeterred. She felt the rhythm of the chase, her pulse syncing with the thunderclaps as she followed each streak of light.

Her fingers traced a delicate pattern in the air and the lights around her shimmered. Her body followed the path of the glowing lines, twisting and turning, bending and shifting with the precision of her movements, she could feel the energy of Kolog beneath her feet, its musical vibrations guiding her as she pursued him. She could hear her trees whispering the ancient songs, their branches swaying in time with her dance.

Just as puffin darted around her, she reached out, her fingers brushing against the edge of his light form. He spun away, a trail of gold and silver trailing behind him, but Lunaara did not give up. Her eyes were locked on him, her body moving with more fluiditiy, more confidence. He started shooting thunders of pale blues across the sky causing ripples of sound in the atmosphere of Kolog.

Puffin's form flickered his light becoming brighter, more erratic, almost as though he were teasing her, daring her to catch him.

You are not even close.

Lunaara smirked, her lips curling into a determined smile. She was close now-So close. She could feel the crackle of energy in the air, her light intertwining with the patterns around her. Every movement she made was more in tune with the rhythm of the chase, the ever shifting dance of light and thunder that Puffin had initiated.

With one final decisive step Lunaara linger forward her body pulsating streaks of shimmering violet, gold and deep crimson and for the first time she caught him. Her fingers brushed against his brilliant light and the energy around them flared with a burst of electricity. The thunder rolled, the air hummed with the resonance of the moment. And for a brief second, everything seemed to freeze.

Puffin's form wavered and then with a sudden flash of light, he spun out of her grasp, darting back into the air with a burst of laughter. He sent out bursts of pink rhythmic lightning bolts and light of electric blue in the air forming smileys.

You did it. You caught me. And as promised I shall grant you your prize. The co-ordinates.

Lunaara now began to pulsate mix rainbow colors forming random patterns.

So where is my prize?

Puffin now shot bolts of electric pink, green, purple and violet on the inverted trees, the musical lands and the solid looking but liquid feeling mountains. Making visual patterns of sound vibrations.

The price has always been all around you Lunaara. You have to listen. Hear what Kolog has been trying to tell you all along.

With this the musical hum of Kolog began to deepen, the trees dancing but this time they made sense as if singing a lullaby.

Puffin now sent out tiny burst of neon pink and orange forming patterns of galaxies and universes also making visual patterns of sound waves.

Listen Lunaara, Listen to the lights and patterns. It is the universe's way of communication. The universe speaks in multiple ways, it speaks in music, dance, light, pattern, colors, sounds, aura's.

Lunaara closed her eyes, letting the music of Kolog, the light and pattern of the universe sink in letting her open her senses. Kolog's music had always been a subtle undercurrent-Something playful, something light but now as Puffin had mentioned, there more to it than just that.

Her mind now opened, and the patterns began to emerge. The world around her shifted, no longer just a play of light and pattern but a language too intricate for words. She could see it now. There in the faintest pulse of light, the co-ordinates. The path to the Cosmic Wrap. They weren't numbers, they weren't simply points on a map. They were a sequence, a flow, a movement-woven into the very fabric of Kolog.

Lunaara opened her eyes and Puffin was waiting, his form now a gentle white. She felt the shift in the air, the weight of the movement and the essence of something greater than she had anticipated.

Her body now pulsating in colors of bright green and dark green forming patterns of a sparkly bridge.

The co-ordinates, they lie in the music of Kolog.

A happy Puffin now bursts outwards electric green and orange forming patterns of music notes in the air.

Exactly the co-ordinates lie in the music of Kolog.

Lunaara was now a little angry hence shoots arrows of dark red and crimson aiming at Puffin while making strong patterns of question marks.

So why the chase?

Puffin ducked these arrows and replied by sending constant long ripples of bright yellow and pink lights.

A test to your resilience. And now that you have unlocked the co-ordinates. Lets hurry to cosmic wrap.

Chapter 16: The first encounter

The Astryn's pulsed with fractured lights as they, along with Lunaara and Puffin arrived at the Cosmic Wrap.

The air was heavy, compressing.

A deep low hum throbbed beneath the surface of reality- A Vibration that didn't Just scrape the mind, but one that got on to the nerves. The cosmic wrap Hovered at the edge of the known universe, a convergence of light and shadow where existence was as fragile as a glass.

The fractured lights of the Astryns shimmered weakly against the oppressive Weight of the atmosphere. Their golden and sapphire hues, normally vibrant And Fluid, faltered patterns, their triangular forms beginning to snap like cracked mirrors. Puffin fluttered unevenly; His chest rose and fell throwing Random sprinkles of lighting.

The void in front of them shifted. Thin slender waves of darkness slithered outwards twisting through the atmosphere like splintered roots.

And then-She arrived.

Drakaara emerged from the fracture-A silhouette of darkness. Her hands folded behind her, her body upright like a walking pole, she walked graciously Towards the Astryns and Lunaara. Her movements were calm. Deliberate.

She stepped forward towards the Astryn's and then

She bowed.

Her dark spirals softened into fluid arcs. Her form knelt slightly, head lowering towards the Astryns.

Moments later she took a step back and with a show of her hands she formed long pitch black patterns of dancing lines which slowly but began forming 4 waves of circle with circles.

"It has been… too long"

The Astryn's pulses tightened. Spitting out lights of Gold and Sapphire hues forming sharp but narrow defensive spirals.

"Now is your time, to surrender"

Lunaara's glow sharpened, she sent out pulses of sharp deep pinks and red which eventually formed patterns of pitch black snakes.

"Drakaara, you need to stop!"

Drakaara now for the first time turns her gaze towards Lunaara, raises her hand and with a show of her hands forms deep obsidian black through the void along with erratically charges pulses of blue like veins cracking through a dying star. The black waves throb-slow at first-before shuddering violently. Then a sudden stillness follows retreating slightly as if recoiling from its own question.

"You have finally arrived Lunaara after all this time but you should not have come. And what is there to stop?"

Lunaara's body now pulsed sharply in mixed random patterns of Yellow, Green and white.

"We will not let you destroy the universe"

Drakaara's spirals darkened further coiling inwards like venomous tendrils. Her Forming patterns of pitch black voids, curling into jagged loops that hissed through the air.

"Destroy?" I am not destroying. I am simply returning the universe to its original form.

The Astryns pulsed in response strong vibrant beams of light forming patterns of a weird mix circles, triangles and squares.

Light and magic are not flaws. They are balance.

Drakaara now lifts her hands and shoots lasers of sharp crimson tearing into the void around them before dissolving into thin, trembling strands of rippling Gold which twists, shivers and then collapses –swallowed by a creeping shadow.

Light is merely a flame, flickering, fleeting-A whisper of fire yet it is the darkness which ignites desire.

Puffin stood like a mute spectator watching patterns of light and dark blending into each other crashing at the edges like opposites.

While the Astryn's pulses tightened. Thin arcs of Neon Golden Lights crackled the air, spiraling towards Drakaara's dark patterns.

"It is not too late, too stop!"

Lunaara now threw waves after waves of strong blues and whites hurling towards Drakaara which began to form patterns of eggs.

"Light is balance, restoration, creation"

Drakaara's spirals darkened. Her dark arcs hissed against Lunaara's light, creating fractures in the surrounding atmosphere.

"Look around you, this, this is Balance"

Lunaara and Astyrns'light patterns pulsed together, forming a bright cascade of Rainbow colored spirals that hovered over the void. Their golden and sapphire pulses expanded outward, forming thin radiant veins of light that spread through the fractured atmosphere.

"There was balance, there was order now there is chaos"

Drakaara's spiral shuddered. Her dark patterns split into fractured, serrated shapes. While forming patterns of black and grey skulls.

"Light is an illusion. Order a fragile dream. The universe plays in the hands of chaos step aside, for resistance is futile."

Lunaara's now spit out flickered violent deep silvers, cream and red lights. Her light spiraled upwards curling through the dark void. Her eyes now turned red, her wings flapped in all her glory.

"Then let us teach you what order truly means."

A sphere of searing white plasma formed between Lunaar's hands, its silver light pulsing through the void. She thrust her arms forward-The Plasma Bombs shot towards Drakaara, cutting through the dark like a streak of violent starlight.

Drakaara countered this with her **"VOIDBEAM GAZE**", her eyes narrowed, twin beams of violet-black light lancing from her pupils. The beams struck the plasma bombs-twisting around it, absorbing the light- Until the bomb collapsed inward. The explosion sent ripples of silver and black spiraling through the void, but Drakaara stood unscathed. Wisps of silver light curled around her before dissolving into the dark.

Lunaara's breath sharpened. She raised her hand. Three Jagged spears of Moonlight spiraled into existence around her. Their silver edges vibrated with unstable energy. Lunaara's eyes flashed- As the **"Lunaar Spear"** shot Towards Drakaara, cutting through the dark in a deadly arc.

Drakaara's hand flickered upward-Black poles of jagged "**Obsidian Spires"** Erupted from the void. The first two spears shattered upon impact, splinters of Silver and Black scattering into the dark. The third spear twisted mid-glight0 but Drakaara eyes glinted darkly.

The obsidian poles twisted toward Lunaara , the sharp tips mere inches from her shoulders.

And that's when the Nebula Shroud struck the mist, dissolving into black dust as the shroud absorbed the impact. The waves of cosmic veil curled protectively around Lunaara.

Drakaara's lips curled dark mist swirled around her-Twisting into a jagged black lance crowned with ghostly skulls. Drakaara hurled it forward-The skulls screamed as the "**Skull Storm Lance"** tore through the void. It stuck the Nebula shroud-The silver mist trembled under the impact-Fractures rippling across its surface from both the skull's physical attack and the intense sound waves.

Lunaara then opened her mouth and released The Eclipse Breath a dark beam of Cosmic energy, it's pure annihilation force cutting through the darkness aiming Straight towards Drakaara hit her at light speed, making her bleed for the first Time since inception. Drakaara bled streams after streams of jet black glitter.

Lunaara thought she had won this fight but this move only angrier Drakaara. In A fit of rage she unleashed **"The Blood storm Fang".**

Drakaara's body pulsed with dark energy and a crimson fang-shaped bolt Erupted from her chest. It spiraled through the space between them, carving a jagged path through the void. The fang slammed into the already broken shroud-The mist shattered in a burst of silver dust.

The shockwaves sent Lunaara reeling.

Draakar blurred into view-Her hand striking out- The tip of a jagged claw slicing across Lunara's side. A thin line of silver blood bloomed along her ribs.

Lunaar's breath hitched. Her knees trembled as pain lanced through her body momentarily as her body began to regenerate a gift from the earlier encounter at the Eclipse Veil.

Drakaara was now taken aback, this was not what she was expecting. In that Moment she had gained a realization. A realization that Lunaara was no ordinary celestial she was special. And this battle is far from over.

Chapter 17: Animal Instinct

The battle was far from over, but the energy around them was thick. Drakaara's Presence still pulsating through the void. Lunaara could feel the dark energy Swirl and shift around her, a break in the battle, a constant, oppressive force.

Drakaara's dark patterns danced in the space around her, twisting and spiraling. An ever moving mass of shadows. They were alive, reflecting the malice that Dripped from Drakaara's every thought. The patterns that twisted in jagged Lines and spirals, like claws scrapping across the universe itself. Each Movement she made sent ripples of darkness towards Lunaara, closing in on her with ferocious speed.

It wasn't just the force of the shadows that stung-no, Drakaara was mocking her. Lunaara could feel the contempt in the twisted patterns, each one a silent Taunt, each curve of the dark lines a reminder of her helplessness. It was as if Drakaara was savoring the moment, toying with Lunaara like a cat with its prey. The patterns spread, outwards, dark threads wrapping tighter and tighter around both her and the Astryn's. Lunaara's own light was dimming under the weight Of Drakaara's mockery.

Lunaara gritted her teeth. Drakaara's silent ridicule was a weapon in itself, one that threatened to unravel her resolve. It was clear that Drakaara sought not just Victory but to break her spirit-to show her that she was merely a speck of dust against the overwhelming power of Darkness.

But Lunaara would not yield. Not yet.

As the dark patterns continued to close in, Lunaara's gaze flickered to the Shadow Pole she could feel it. It was alive, but not in the way she had once known it. The pole, once a powerful conduit between the realms, was now an Insatiable drain on the universe itself. Its tendrils stretched far beyond her reach,

Draining the very essence of light, life and energy into grasp.

Lunaara could sense it with every fiber of her being-The Shadow Pole was pulling at the fabric of existence. It was draining the very lifeblood of the universe. Stars were losing their flicker, planets were losing their shine, slowly but truly the universe was turning into a cosmic graveyard. The very life Source of the universe was being sucked into it, feeding its hunger for power. It was consuming everything about it. The universe was dying in its grasp. The Weight of the revelation struck her. If the pole continued to feed, there would be Nothing left-No light, no wonder, no magic-no creatures, no stars, no beings, no Planets nothing but darkness. A welcoming, suffocating darkness. A never Ending void. The shadow pole's power had become a primal cosmic force, one that could not be easily undone.

Her heart pounded in her chest, the urgency of the moment settling into every Bone of her body, she could no longer wait. The moments of hesitation had passed.

Her instincts surged to the forefront. A wave of primal energy washed over her, not guided by thought but by pure instinct-The instinct of a predator facing the End of the hunt. Lunaara's every movement became fluid, her body reacting to the pull of her instincts.

She didn't think, she just moved.

Without hesitation she ran towards the shadow pole. It was like the instinct of an animal that knew only survival-Everything else was secondary, she ran her Body sleek and swift and in a flash, she reached the pole, there was no time for Subtlety or thought. This was a battle of primal instincts of pure raw action.

She opened her mouth wide and sank her teeth into the shadow pole, holding it Tithe every ounce of strength she had. It was cold, smooth-Unnervingly so as Though it was made of something far more ancient and indestructible than anything she had ever encountered. As she clamped down on it, she felt an immediate shock run through her, a violent jolt that made her body convulse. The pole was pulling at her, trying to suck the very essence of her existence into its endless hunger.

Yet she did not let go.

She anchored herself to the pole, using every ounce of strength to uproot it from The Cosmic Wrap. Her body screamed in protest. Every movement sent waves of pain through her as the pole drained her energy, as if it were trying to consume her very being but she held firm, knowing there was no other choice. She had to uproot it. She had to destroy it before it was too late.

The pain grew unbearable, the pull of the Shadow Pole overwhelming. Lunaara could feel her body weakening, her energy draining away, slipping through her Grasp like water in the wind. Her vision blurred, the edges of her consciousness fading as if she were slipping into unconsciousness.

It was then that the Astryn's acted.

With a powerful surge of energy, the Astryn's gathered around her, their diamond forms glowing brightly against the dark void. Their bodies flickered with light, each movement sharp and precise. With a wave of their hands, The Astryn's directed their power towards the Shadow Pole, weakening it temporarily. Lunaara could feel the balance shift, the crushing force of pole's Hunger softening just enough for her to hold on.

The Astryn's energy poured into the pole. Their light weakening it and counteracting its pull. They knew what they had to do. With coordinated Precision, the Astryn's channeled their collective power into a single, focused Burst, the pole which had been deeply entwined with the Cosmic Wrap began to Shift, pulling free from its grip. The Astryn's using their light, pulled it from its Dark binding.

It was a violent release. The pole screaming as it tore free from its place, causing ripples in the fabric of space. The struggle between light and dark was palpable, but in that moment, Lunaara and Astryns had the upper hand.

Her body still ached, the pain unbearable, but the pole was finally out, in her Mouth. And with that came a brief moment of calm.

The Astryn's did not pause, with the pole now free, one of them, Puffin stepped forward. His tiny form gleamed as he focused his energy with a chirpy smile. The space around them shimmered and a white portal began to open-bright Radiant white and full of lightning bolts. On the other end was Kolog. The Astryns, knowing the risks acted quickly.

Lunaara too weak to stand, was lifted by the combined force of the Astryns. She could steel feel the shadows closing in, the last remnants of Drakaara's dark Power lingering like a threat on her consciousness. But they were no longer in the void. The portal shimmered before her, a final escape from the dark, a Chance to return back to home, back to Kolog.

With one last effort, puffin's power surged completing the opening of the portal. It was a doorway- A Safe passage back to Kolog, the only place they could rest and regroup.

With another thought Lunaara let herself be pulled into the light. The Cosmic Wrap was now left behind her, its weight and malice no longer pressing down on her. She felt the rush of magic envelop her as the portal closed behind them sealing off the dark space.

They had escaped with the Shadow Pole still in between Lunaara's teeth, Leaving Drakaara in rage.

The Void trembled with Drakaara's fury. The space where Lunaara, Puffin and The Astryn's had vanished still crackled with residual energy, the last Shimmering traces of Puffin's portal mocking her like distant laughter. Her Shadow twisted, violently trashing against nothingness. Clawing at the Remnants of a battle she had not yet finished with yet the Shadow Pole was Gone.

With deep rage in her eyes, Drakaara began. She extended her arms, pulling the dust from the air the dead remnants of the frozen, lifeless particles of the stars and planets previously captured in her paintings gathered in a swirling mass before her. Each fragment seemed to pulse with an eerie light of its own. The energy of countless lost planets and stars now serving a single purpose to locate Kolog.

She raised her hands high and the dust began to spin in a spiraling vortex. The dead planets and star's energies surged and hummed, almost alive with the echoes of their once glorious existence. She summoned their energies through a deep, wordless thought while casting a spell on each of these energies.

The dust twisted and formed into patterns, each moving to the beat of a rhythm only Drakaara understood. She began to weave these energies into a magical glowing dark dust creating a spiral of absolute dark energy. As the dust touched these long lost planets and stars they seemed to shudder as if waking from a deep slumber. Their surfaces now crackled emitting a ghostly glow. As they absorbed the energy of the dead worlds around them.

With her will focused, Drakaara sent these energies into every direction of the vast emptiness of the space, sending them out like boomerangs of forgotten light and energy in search of the co-ordinates she needed. The only way to locate the Kaelyon Constellation.

The frozen lifeless particles of planets and stars locked in a spell moved through space in a trance but this time with an eerie glow flashing against the void like cold, dead lanterns. Each of them bound to return like echoes lost in the endless night. As they moved they left a trail of shimmering star skulls, a path only visible to Drakaara. The dead planet and stars have guided her right to Kolog.

Chapter 18: The revelation

The Astryns stood in solemn stillness, their diamond bodies catching the faint Iridescence of Kolog's lights. Then with a pulse of refracted brilliance, their Communication began- A silent symphony of intricate, shifting light patterns that danced in the air like an unspoken hymn.

The First Astryn shot up a spiral unfurled delicate yet resolute lights of blues, violets, and whites towards Lunaara-A symbol of respect, an acknowledgement of the battle well fought.

"You fought well"

Lunaara's glow flickered dim and uneven, yet her response was deliberate, concentric circles expanding weakly in lights of pale yellow and green from her core, mirroring the message the Astryn had sent.

"You taught well"

The rings of lights quivered as they traced memories-Their teachings, the Lessons carved into very essence of her being. She had not only wielded power but had shaped it with wisdom, the wisdom they had given her.

The second Astryn watched her waning light. A new sequence took form-Angular, yet fluid, shifting in measured rhythm shot towards Lunaara in lights of light pink and red.

"Rest, let the light return to you"

Lunaara hesitated, a final, faint pulse escaped her- The quiet acknowledgment of their command. And then surrendering to the silent embrace of Regeneration, Her glow receded like a dying ember and she drifted into deep Slumber.

Lunaara's body lay motionless upon the ever-humming surface of Kolog, her Luminescence reduced to a faint whisper while the essence of her being stirred. Lunaara was now realizing the decision she took by exchanging her innocence in exchange of regenerative abilities where now coming handy.

Now she was immortal but yes she was exhausted. Exhausted from the intense fight with Drakaara, exhausted by the intense pull from the Shadow Pole. The Power of Eclipse Veil did not merely heal-It restored. As she rested, her energy did not only return, it reformed like the quiet mending of cosmic fractures.

The Astryns stood as silent spectators, their bodies reflecting the glow of Kolog's inverted trees, waiting. Waiting for the rebirth of her brilliance.

Above them the pink skies swirled in slow, endless motion. A canvas of spectral Hues as though Kolog itself mirrored the movement of Lunaara's soul.

And still she slept.

The Astryns turned their attention to the Shadow Pole now letting Lunaara rest And recover. It stood tall. Obsidian, absolute. A monolith of stolen creation, the Creation, the light, the stars, the planets that were imprisoned. It was still pulsating from within its core.

Both the Astyn's now combined together and shot a surge of refracted force that Rippled through the air aiming at the Shadow Pole. The attack was a concentrated blast of energy, weaving intricate fractals of luminous destruction.

The attack met the surface of the pole-But nothing, not a crack, not a tremor.

Again they struck. This time a synchronized sequence, their diamond limbs Shifting into a unified prism of condensed power. A blast of purest energy Cascaded against the Shadow Pole, illuminating the darkness in a dazzling form of shattered colors.

Still, the pole remained untouched.

It did not resist, it did not absorb. It simply endured.

The Astryns pulsed in growing urgency their Dark red and Crimson lights forming sharp, jagged Patterns of frustration.

"This is not possible"

And that's when the air crackled. A rolling chuckle of thunder and mischief. It Was Puffin.

A tiny wispy mass of storm hovered before them, its shape shifting between Delicate vapor and playful sparks of electricity. Puffin swirled with glee, his Presence light as air, yet carrying the weight of knowledge as old as the stars.

"Your efforts are futile, Strike it? Shatter It? The shadow pole does not work That way"

The Astryns turned their prismatic gazes towards him, Shooting out orange and blue lights forming mixed waves of patterns which made no sense towards Puffin.

"Explain"

Puffin flickered bouncing mid air releasing soft crackles of lighting and thunder.

"The Shadow Pole" cannot be broken, the universe that has been imprisoned Can only be released"

He drifted closer to the pole. The electric wisps of his form crackling against its Surface. A spark. A gleam. A knowing glint in his ever lightning cloud body.

"And to release this you need something primal."

The Astryn's looked at each other before sending zigzagged patterns of multiple Neon blues, oranges, yellows and greens before finally forming broken triangles Shot towards Puffin.

"Something primal? Like what?"

Puffin in response shout out a long lightning bolt in the sky which then blasted to Make a huge pattern of sparkly golden mandala.

"A chant"

In response to these both the Astryn's shot bright yellow lights and bright white Lights making incomplete Mandala's towards Puffin.

"A chant?"

Puffin now shots multiple thunder bolts of electricity in the sky which later formed patterns of stars, galaxies, and planets. These patterns stayed still long Before disappearing.

"The First chant of the universe. The chant that woke creation itself. The Chant That called first light of the universe. And only one being in the entire universe Still carries that chant in his soul."

In response to this the Astryns shot out bright white and gold lights forming Patterns of spirals of Star Dust.

"Who?"

Puffin then let out thunders and lightning bolts making patterns of rolling Storms which later burst out into random spots of vibrant gold and silvers like Random dots in the universe.

"Nerion-The cosmic traveler.

The realization settled in. The patterns of the Astryns have flickered throughout Their own body as their mind was thinking.

"If this was true, then-Junkin-The planet of Eldarion."

They shifted, their bright green, brown and yellow lights making holographic patterns of Eladrion projected right towards Puffin.

"If the first chant created The universe, then Eldarion must know it. We must seek him."

Puffin let out a burst of static laughter, he swirled in the air spinning playfully. With every laughter, the static the thunder bolts changed colors from static White to static Blue and then a pause, a hum of deepening Electricity.

"Very noble, very predictable but very wrong"

The Astryn's now shot out lights of light green and bright white making patterns of semi spirals

"Why?"

Puffin crackled, his wisps growing dark at the edges, as though even the storms feared the truth.

"Because the chant didn't belong to Eladarion, it abandoned him the Moment he settled in Junkin, the moment he stopped moving"

He then spun shooting scary serious long thunder bolts of static gold and blues forming Patterns of the Eladrion's diamond body which later burst into the Mandala Again.

"Eldarion never created the chant, the chant created Eldarion and Nerion was His first creation but he refused to settle. Eladarion only found it and used to Shape the universe."

The Astryn's then send a mix of rainbow lights forming patterns of waves Which then exploded into absolute random patterns.

"But then why did the chant abandon Eladarion, why can't he no longer Use it?"

Puffin sighed and swirled but this in absolute slow motion throwing out soft Lightning bolts of gold and silvers which erupted into straight lights made of Glowing stardust.

"Because the universe, it loves momentum, movement. It doesn't, it cannot Survive in stagnancy. It falls in love with wanderers with crazy hearts, the Drifters who never settled, never stayed in one place for long."

Exactly then the sky above them rumbled as if the universe itself had spoken.

After a long moment of silence. The second Astryn replied by shooting bright Pink, Blues, Oranges making rising and falling waves which combined with each other to make holographic image of Lunaara and Puffin which then burst into Random bursts of dots like random dots in the universe.

Since Nerion is constantly on the move, since he is the cosmic traveler you And Lunaara leave in his search of him while we(Referring to the other Astryn) stay back guarding Kolog.

The first Astryn agrees and shoots lights of Bright green, gold, and static blue Making patterns of dark tendrils which then burst into patterns of empty dark canvasses.

"I agree, Drakaara must already be on his way to Kolog, she will not sit quiet. Bring Nerion here so he can project the chant at the Shadow Pole."

Puffin in response smiles and swirls leaving random bursts of lightning all Across Kolog.

"Absolutely"

A low hum filled the air as Puffin swirled in a lazy loop above Lunaara, his tiny Form crackling with playful mischief. He hovered closer, releasing a quick Pulse of static that danced across her dormant glow. When she didn't stir, he Flickered with impatience and she sent a small jolt of lightning right at her trail.

Still nothing.

With an exaggerated sigh, Puffin shot up gathered a storm of electric threads Around him and then-Boom!-Unleashed a sharp clap of thunder that rippled Through the skies.

Lunaara woke up flickered with a slow deliberate pulse- She stretched like a Dog- Her entire form radiating with renewed energy, By the time her eyes fully Opened, the remnants of exhaustion had already faded. She even didn't even seemed annoyed instead her glow rippled in strong, confident waves, charged, whole, and ready.

Puffin twirled midair, satisfied then without wasting a moment, he lifted a Crackling limb to the sky and let a series of charged bolts carve their way Through the sky. The patterns they formed were sharp deliberate-A story Written in lightning.

"We need to move, you and I will find Nerion-The Cosmic Traveler while the Astryn's will stay behind safeguarding Kolog from Draakara"

Lunaara then opened her mouth and shot lights of Crimson, red and sparkly Purple, forming patterns of spirals after spirals intertwined with one another.

"Nerion? Who? And why do we need to find him?"

Puffin spun in the air once more and send a final single strike which burned Bright before vanishing into the abyss then shout out

long waves of lightning bolts after bolts in the sky creating patterns of galaxies, planets and stars which broke into random dots.

“Nerion is the only being in the universe that still carries the first chant of the universe, which is required to release the prisoners of the Shadow Pole.”

Lunaara now charged with excitement sent out waves of Rainbow lights forging Strong sword like patterns.

“If that is the case, then lets hurry”.

Chapter 19: Nerion

At the heart of Kolog a tiny figure stood. Puffin, the little 3 ounce cloud floating Just above the ground, his usually carefree form now heavy with purpose, His Cloudy hands, barely tangible, pressed together in a solemn prayer. His eyes +-Two flickering sparks of lightning-were closed, his tiny mouth whispering silent Pleas in an ancient language of crackling thunder.

As he prayed minute thunderbolts-delicate yet powerful-leapt from his Form,

Spiraling into the heavens. The sky responded rumbling as if the very fabric of The cosmos acknowledged the call. Lunaara towering beside him, watched in Quiet reverence. Her form once battle worn and drained, now stood tall, she Remained silent understanding this was a scared moment for Puffin.

The winds grew restless, the rainbow falls halted mid air, each droplet as if Frozen awaiting the arrival of something ancient and immense. Then with a Deep cosmic sigh, space itself seemed to part. From the Abyss beyond the skies, A shadow darker than void took form.

The Hollow Star Descended.

It was unlike anything bound by mortal logic.-A celestial husk, An abandoned Vessel of forgotten light. Its form was a fractured sphere, vast yet weightless Hollow at its core. Its outer shell was made of cosmic obsidian, rippling with Remnants of past supernovas. Shattered fragments of stardust drifted around it Like a halo, glowing faintly, whispering echoes of the moments when it had Once burned with life.

As the hollow star drew closer, its blackened surface pulsed in responding to Puffin's thunderous prayers. The once-lost relic had heard its summoner. It was Awake.

Puffin slowly opened his eyes. A knowing smile formed on his misty face. He Shot short burst of lightning form arrow like patterns into the sky which then Burst into random sparkling dots.

"Let's go"

The journey had begun.

Yet as the hollow star hovered before the, a deep stillness filled the air. It was Not mere silence-It was the weight of an entity that had seen the birth and death Of countless realms. The sphere's surface shifted slightly, reflecting the glow of Kolog's inverted floating trees in its fractured glass-like body. Each crack, each Imperfection, told a story of forgotten wars between celestial beings, of stars That once burned bright but had long since faded into nothingness.

Lunaara stepped forward, she raised her head slightly, peering into the abyss Within. There was something… familiar about it. A strange pull as if the Remnants of lost galaxies still whispered within its core.

She shot out a combination of white and black lights sending ripples of Moonlight making patterns of stars which burst into patterns of random waves.

"Is, is this… Alive"?

Puffin glanced at her, then back at the Hollow Star. A gust of cold wind swirled Around them, Carrying the scent of ancient dust. He then shot out static blue And static white lightning bolts which intertwined and formed patterns of Blurry galaxies, stars and planets.

"No but it remembers"

Lunaara took a step forward her hooves barely making a sound against the soft, Musical land. The melody beneath them shifted, a quiet hum vibrating through The land, as if Kolog itself acknowledged the momentous journey about to Begin.

Puffin floated ahead, his tiny form barely a whisper against the vastness of the Hollow Star. His tiny little hands sending a final pulse of electric energy Towards the celestial vessel. The cracks upon its surface shimmered in Response, the dark, obsidian-like material pulsing as if breathing for the first Time in ages.

A narrow opening appeared in on its side-Not a door, not an entryway, but a Tear in its very being. It revealed an interior that seemed both infinite and Confined shifting between dimensions as though undecided on what it should Be. The walls were not sold, they were remnants of collapsed stars, their dying Light trapped within,

Lunaara hesitated for a moment. This was no ordinary journey. The vessel-this Hollow Star was a relic of a forgotten age. To step inside was to step into the Remnants of something beyond her understanding.

Puffin sensing her hesitation, turned back his tiny hands, still cracked with soft Thunder, reached of hers. His lightning bolts now lacking its usual mischievous Sparkles forming pattern of straight white static lightning Towards the hollow star.

"We need to go"

Lunaara looked at him. In that moment, the tiny cloud looked different. Not just A playful whips of energy, but something more-Something ancient, something Powerful in its own right.

She exhaled a breath of silver mist and nodded.

Stepping forward, she placed her hoof against the hollow star's surface. A ripple Spread outwards, shifting the fractured reflections of the universe trapped Within. The moment her full form passed through the opening, the void inside The Vessel shifted, recognizing her presence. The star's internal structure Resembling a path, though it was made of nothing but floating light and Shadow.

Puffin followed, his small form leaving behind trails of golden sparks as he Drifted beside her. The moment he entered, the hollow star shuddered and the Tear they had stepped through stitched itself back together, sealing them inside.

Then, without a single sound it began to move.

From the outside of the hollow star looked unchanged-Floating still in the Endless sky of Kolog. But within Lunaara and Puffin could feel it-The shifting Pull of the universe around them, the weight of the unseen forces guiding Toward something unknown.

Puffin closed his eyes again, his tiny hands glowing.

It was time to command their vessel. He then extended a hand and from his Fingertips, a pulse of soft, crackling light danced outward stretching towards the Far end of the Hollow Star.

The ancient vessel groaned in response, shifting its course towards the Unknown.

The search for Nerion had begun.

The hollow star did not move through space like a conventional vessel; It Responded to the light signals given to it. Whenever Puffin or Lunaara released a stream of light, the hollow star aligned itself with it, seamlessly shifting in that Direction. It did not accelerate, nor did it drift aimlessly-it simply became part Of the path illuminated before it. The vessel was neither alive nor dead, neither Mechanical not organic yet it obeyed light with an eerie precision.

With the mechanism now understood, Lunaara and Puffin focused on their Search. They traversed through the remaining of what was once a thriving Universe-now a graveyard of forgotten stars and shattered celestial bodies. Darkness sprawled endlessly around them, a near- void punctuated only by Remnants of light clinging desperately to existence.

Massive planetary husks floated in the abyss stripped of their atmospheres, Reduced to skeletal remains. Cracked moons, hollowed out from within, and Loomed like ghostly eyes staring into infinity. There was no warmth here, no Energy, only the silent echoes of creation that once was.

Puffin's gaze was sharp, her eyes scanning for any trace of Nerion. He was a Being of eternal frost, a wandered of the void and if he still existed. His Presence would be felt in the air itself. He then floated beside Lunaara releasing Tiny streaks of static white light bolts that arched through the void illuminating the ruins of forgotten realms. The energy danced across lifeless Asteroids, flickering off their frozen surfaces before fading into nothingness.

A faint in shimmer in the distance caught Lunaara's eye. It was subtle, almost Imperceptible, like a breath of frost lingering in the air, her pulse quickened, eyes widened. She then shot out lights of

jagged yellow which later turned to Orange through her own body forming patterns of random asteroids, and galaxies.

"Can this be him? Can this be the Cosmic Traveler?"

Puffin immediately extended a pulse of gold and white static lightning bolts Towards the shimmer, The Hollow Star reacted, gliding towards it in eerie Silence.

The air grew colder. Not the kind of cold that burned out but a cold that was Ancient-As if it belonged to the first breaths of existence itself. Lunaara inhaled Sharply.

They were close.

As the Hollow Star drifted closer, the shimmer in the void expanded, unraveling Into delicate fractals of frost. The air itself seemed to crystallize forming Intricate patterns that hung momentarily before dissolving back into the abyss. Lunaara and Puffin watched in silence as the space before them bent- not like a Portal, not like a tear in reality, but as if something was walking from a sleep so Deep that even the universe had forgotten it.

A low hum resonated through the emptiness vibrating through the Hollow Star's Hollow shell. It wasn't a sound-It was presence. A feeling that rippled through Their very existence.

Then from the center of the Shimmering frost, he emerged.

Nerion.

He did not step forward, nor did he materialize. He simply was. His body Sculpted from thick white transparent ice. His form was not jagged or rough but Impossibly smooth like glass frozen in divine stillness. And behind him trailing Like a celestial whisper was a stream of sparkling frost-An ever present aura That made the darkness itself appears alive.

His face, if one could call it that was never still. It shifted like a puzzle in Motion, no fixed expression-Only the ceaseless shifting of an ever-changing Visage.

Puffin despite his usual carefree nature, remained motionless in this sacred Silence. Lunaara however took a step forward, absorbing every detail of the Being before her.

Nerion did not speak, he did not need to instead his entire form pulsed-Light Cascading outward in rhythmic sequences, each hue and movement layered with Meaning. Lights of yellow, orange, bright greens twisting and hurling Intertwining to form patterns of constellations, galaxies, asteroids.

"You gave come searching for me"

A pause. A flicker of deep blue followed by a slow ripple of silver.

"But why?"

Lunaara's shot out steady lights of crimson, velvet and red which later bursts into patens of broken asteroids, moon, galaxies and stars

"Because the universe is breathings its last."

Puffin then from the wave of his tiny hands made long thunderbolts Resembling That of the shadow pole however more a sparkly, more vibrant version of its Which then broke into tiny particles aiming it towards Nerion.

"You are the only one who can break the shadow pole"

For a moment, there was no response. Then, Nerion's form pulsed again-This Time, a slow rhythmic undulating wave of violet and white forming Circular waves.

"It can only be broken using the first chant of the universe".

Lunaara then shot out straight lights of Purple, indigo and green towards Nerion Which broke into pyramid like triangles.

"That is what brings us to you. Only you can save the universe."

Nerion's shifting face paused-Just for a fraction of a second. Then for the first Time in eternity, the frost surrounding him softened.

Nerion did not like to stay at one place but then the vast near dead universe Held its breath as hard as it could. Nerion loved the universe even more than he Loved his travels across it. And no universe would mean no more travels.

Nerion's shimmering frost extended outward, spiraling through the darkness Like a celestial river. Then with a slow, deliberate movement, his entire being Radiated a luminous white-Purer, brighter than any light Lunaara had ever Witnessed.

A soft breeze though impossible in space, stirred the edges of reality itself. It Carried with it a presence-Something ancient, something even beyond the Oldest stars.

Lunaara and Puffin exchanged a glance. They knew.

Nerion has decided.

With a slow soundless motion, he turned towards them. His entire being Emanating layered sequence of light and color.

"Take me to the Shadow Pole"

Without hesitating Puffin raised her tiny hand, sending out a pulse of guiding Lightning bolts. The hollow star attuned to her will, responded instantly-Its Dark, skeletal Frame humming as it adjusted course. The stars they had passed Each in their search now rushed past them in reverse these time landing straight Back to Kolog.

Back at Kolog, the Astryn's for the first time in eternity bowed to a creature Apart from Eladrion, they bowed to Nerion. The Astryn guided him to the Shadow Pole.

Nerion for the first time was witnessing the shadow pole. A towering void Neither light nor dark something in between. He could see the trapped galaxies, Whispers of civilizations, screams of the fading lights only making him Angry.

His urge to stomp the pole, to break it, to smash it was as aggressive as the Suns however he knew these efforts prove futile as only the first chant of the Universe can break the pole.

So he moved, drifted towards the pole leaving behind a trail of shimmering frost On the musical lands of Kolog. As he neared the pole, his lights grew more Complex, more intricate-Patterns upon patterns layered like the verses of a Divine poem and then with a single deliberate motion, he directed his lights Towards the pole.

The effect was immediate.

The Shadow Pole began trembled.

Cracks of luminescence splintered through its form, like lightning fracturing the Deepest night. The imprisoned echoes of civilizations shuddered as light wove Through them, unbinding the chains of entropy that had kept them frozen in Oblivion. One by one, the whispers of the forgotten became voices again. One By One the shattered fragrance of lost creation flickered back into existence.

The universe breathed again.

Lunaara watched as the impossible unfolded before her. Stars that had been Extinguished reignited, galaxies long abandoned to darkness found their constellations again. Crystallium, Emrithar, Pulsitar regained their light, life and Magic once again, they were back to their original coordinates, the silent void That had choked the cosmos began to unravel, replaced by slow rhythmic hum Of creation.

Puffin floated beside Nerion, let out waves after waves of thunderbolts and Lightning mixed with static golden sparkles- A way of happiness.

Lunaara exhaled softly, her gaze locked on Nerion as he lingered in the space Where the pole had once loomed. His frost still shimmering, his face still Shifting but now his light held something new, something gentle. Something Like peace.

While Lunaara, Nerion and Puffin celebrated. The Astryn's were worried. They Were worried about Drakaara. About why she didn't come after the pole, this is Unlike of her.

Was she making her next move? Or had she already begun?

Chapter 20: Zolo

Situated in the southwestern quadrant of Kolog, precisely at coordinate's k-27 Degree s,y-56 degree E rests the city of Zolo- A place unlike any other. The city Thrives with a slimy basin surrounded by the bioluminescent trees that hum Softly with energy. Zolo is a celebration of softness, glow and boundless joy. It Has never known what sadness feels like. Its air smells sweet and its lands Squishes comforting with each step.

Zolo is home to the **Zelapphariums**-Enigmatic beings made entirely of sentient Jelly. No two Zelphariums looks alike: each carries a unique color, texture and Consistency of gelatinous form. The only exceptions are the rare Zelpharium Twins, whose identical hues make them minor celebrities in the community.

They do not communicate with words, instead they exchange **Chemical Melodies**-Bio chemical pulses that emit fragrances, colors and subtle vibrations, Each composition carrying layered meanings. When one Zelpharium sings, Another inhales and understanding blooms. These melodies are visible as Floating spirals of scent-light that twist and dance between beings like playful Smoke.

Structures in Zolo are not made from bricks or crystals but from hardened jelly That grows from the land itself, shaped by generations of touch and memory. Tall, twisting towers resembling giant dripping candles and bridges stretch like Lazy tongues over glimmering lakes of syrupy water.

The city pulses with collective laughter and rhythm as if joy itself were Embedded in its foundation. Zolo is never still-It undulates, breathes and Responds to its inhabitants.

Though they lack weapons or defenses they have never needed them. There has Never been war. There has never been betrayal. Their city has never been Touched by grief, fear or suspicion. In Zolo even the nights are Luminous.

But Zolo's beauty has never been its design or its inhabitants- It has always Been their unwavering innocence. That joy, eternal and unmarred, the very Blessing Drakaara now seeks to corrupt.

Far beyond Zolo's slimy borders. Stood Drakaara, waiting, observing as deceit Would be instantly noticeable in the Joyous bloom of Zolo. So she shed it.

She condensed her existence, folding her vast power into something nearly Invisible-A micro form no larger than an earth ant. This newly adopted form Was called **"Chytroph",** An insignificant speck that moved through slime Unnoticed. No zelpharium had eyes to see such a minute thing and no chemical Melody could sense it.

In this form, Drakaara slithered and bounced across the gelatinous terrain of Zolo. Every squish of the land beneath her felt foreign. The city smelled of Delight, something that offended her very being, still she endured for this was The best opportunity to destroy the Astryn's from within.

Her microform crawled beneath slimy bridges, between translucent towers, and Past spiraling melodies of Zelphariums laughing in colors. Their innocence Irritated her but also served as the perfect camouflage.

She chose her mark- A solitary Astryn walking through Zolo surveying the city- Part of routine checks.

Drakaara followed , nestling into the folds of slime where even Chemical Melodies couldn't reach. Her movements were careful, rhythmic, echoing the Natural pulsation of Chyroph's. She had become an unseen beat in their Cheerful song.

As the Astryn approached the syrup-lake at the city's edge, Drakaara knew the Moment had come. With the quiet precision of a needle sliding into a fabric, she Uncoiled a darker relic from her microform body.

It was her most dreaded tool- A canvas darker than void, capable of capturing even the Astryn's. This was no ordinary trap, It was downright sinister. It was The **"Nullweave"**- A cursed canvas stitched in silence, using the most ancient, Forbidden, Ghastly spell.

The Astryn paused for just a moment by the lake when Drakaara's microform Surged unfolding likes a blossom of despair. The Nullweave canvas billowed out Silently from her core, swallowing all light within its borders.

The Astryn barely turned his gaze before it happened. A shimmer of motion, a Twist of air- and his form was gone, imprisoned inside the canvas.

The painting pulsed once absorbing the Astryn entirely, embedding his image in Eternal stillness. The canvas shimmered like oil on water, the captured Astryn Suspended mist-stride, eyes widened, trying to break free but forever caught in Motion.

Drakaara recoiled the canvas, compressing it back into her new form. No one Had seen. No Zelpharium noticed. Their melodies danced on oblivious.

With her prey secured Drakaara began the second phase-Perfectly mimicking The captured Astryn-Adopting it's diamond form, its triangular head. Its light Sequence language, its scent, its memories.

She had studied the Astryn's long enough, to wear their skin.

Now disguised as the captured Astryn, Drakaara walked casually through Zolo-No longer a mere speck but a god amongst jelly.

Inside a coiling jelly tower shaped like a frozen spiral wave, Lunaara, Nerion, Puffin and the other Astryn were gathered. The city had offered them its Largest structure for strategic deliberation. The walls pulsed in time with their Breath and the melodies coiled like incense in the air.

Drakaara now posing as the captured Astryn, joined the gathering. Her form Was flawless no one questioned her presence.

The true Astryn shot out spirals of Violet and Cyan blinked into double helixes Which then danced like waves, punctuated by pulses of red that throbbed like Breathing wounds.

"We have won the fight but the battle still remains"

To which Nerion replies by shooting out frozen beams of red and white lights which then erupt Into crystalline patterns of

holographic shield which then Broke into tiny salt like crystals from which emerged pitch black skulls.

"You are right, Drakaara will not keep still after this defeat, we must Attack before she does"

The true Astryn then shot out a single droplet of light- A pinprick of white that Hovered in the pink sky of Kolog silently. Then it exploded in every direction, The light fractured into thousands of filaments, each strand a different hue: Violet that pulsed like a heartbeat, cyan that spiraled like wind, gold that curved Into arcs. The filaments wove together, crisscrossing mid-air to create a circular Mandala, spinning slowly.

Suddenly, that mandala broke apart, and the fragments formed cubes, then Dissolved into thin vertical lines, hovering like falling rain-yet they never Touched the ground.

Within those vertical lights, tiny spinning glyphs emerged-Like eyes blinking Open and then closing in sync forming a cage of hexagonal brilliance made of all 7 colors of rainbow hovering mid air, pulsing like a heartbeat.

"Drakaara is made of darkness itself. Drakaara cannot be shattered but can only Be captured. A prison shall be form not my might but by meditation. **The Light Prison.**

Hence two lights must part ways only to grow in solitude. Me and the other Astryn shall meditate separately. we must not see, not smell, not sense the other Until our light has grown enough to forge the light prison and once we return, Our lights will collide, bend, merge and crystallize to make the light prison, it Will not kill, but it will hold. It will hold the darkness itself, Drakaara itself. While we are in meditation Lunaara, Nerion and Puffin you will guard Kolog. Drakaara might attack us at any moment"

With this the meeting concluded. Drakaara made her next move using the Meditating separately to her advantage she walked through the main Artery of Zolo-The swaying trail, a path made of pulsating slime that led to the heart pond.

She stood in the center of the city where joy was thickest, where chemical Melodies were most radiant. Around her, Zelphariums of all sizes played and Danced spirals of scent-light painting the air.

She opened a fresh dark canvas again.

This time, the canvas bloomed like a black sun, expanding into a vortex of Silence. It drank in the light, the melodies, the colors one by one sucking up Zolo as a whole, The zelphariums vanished, frozen mid-spin, mid-laughter, Mid-song.

But this painting was unlike of her other paintings for even when they after Being captured, they didn't cry, they didn't scream, even in the capture the Zelphariums emitted melodies of joy. They clapped. They twirled.

Their faces if one could call them that were aglow with happiness. Zolo had Never known sadness and even now in the moments of capture sadness seemed Foreign to them.

Drakaara for the first time was unnerved the canvas was filling with color-more Color than ever before. The Zelphariums had turned their prison into a carnival.

Still with the stroke of her brush stained in darkness she sealed her canvas.

Zolo was gone. Trapped yet not broken.

Chapter 21: Whispers of the vanishing cities

As decided in the meeting. Lunaara, Puffin and Nerion parted ways to Guard Kolog. Each choosing a direction of the vast planet to ensure no direction Went Unchecked. No farewell was spoken only an exchange of glances likes a Deal Sealed in their eyes.

Lunaara walked away eastwards, her form casting form over the musical lands Of Kolog. Her body charged after the rest she got earlier, her walk confident. The confidence which came as a result of finding being able to find Nerion Previously. She walked until she reached the first city of the east. A silent path Called **"Silora"** resting at coordinates 24.70 Degree East, 37.88 Degree Kolog . Silora isn't just silent-Its emotionally dormant. A city wrapped in a soft sadness So ancient and still, it doesn't even know it's sad. It simply doesn't know joy-Like an entity born blind to colors that others feel. Its inhabitants- **"The Solari"** creatures made of glassy skin stretched over slow burning embers, Glowing faintly from within. They move like shadows drifting though honey-Each step takes feels like a millennia.

They communicate in **"Memory Drips"** –Slow trails of glowing fluid that trace Emotions along the ground and walls, only to evaporate after minutes of silence. The Buildings are carved from **"Stilled Quartz"** A crystal so dense that it even Seizes movements. The lands hum with the absence of vibration. It's soft, Velvet-like, yet doesn't react to touch or movement.

Lunaara's task was simple: Stay Vigilant.

Nerion the cosmic traveler, took the western belt of Kolog. His presence was Like walking memory leaving behind a trail of shimmering frost. He found Himself in the region of coordinates 71.29 degree west, 12.13 degree kolog In a city called "**Quendrum-A.K.A the city of creation."**In Quendrum every thought-No matter how small, fleeting or strange is heard by the city. And the City responds. If you think of warmth a gold breeze instantly wraps around you. If you think of silence the air immediately becomes still and muffled like snowfall. Think of a floating chair- and it floats around you. Think of home- and a structure rises around you shaped exactly like the home in your thoughts. Its creatures-The "**Quen'drai**" These beings are born from thought-They are Mental artifacts that gained permanence. Some are majestic glowing deers with Words written on them made from the dreams of a poet. Some are disturbing: Legless, Headless shadow-things or creatures with too many eyes-By products Of fear, confusion, or intrusive thoughts. No two Quindrai are the same because No two minds are the same. They don't speak, they don't shoot lights, and neither Do they shot out darkness they communicate through manifested reactions. If They like you flowers bloom on their skin, if they don't they twist into glass. When no one is thinking they freeze like paused ideas.

Puffin whimsical as ever but sharp beneath the surface floated north. The skies Near coordinates 24.77 Degree North,03.91 Degree Kolog buzzed with mirage Visions-This was "Iridome" a city of mirror-pools and spectral flora. Puffin Perched high on a floating petal tower, his eyes reflecting a thousand realities as He kept watch. No movement escaped his iridescent sight.

Communication between the three was minimal. They had agreed: no Distractions, no contact unless necessary. Instead they documented everything They saw in beams of colors-Green for peace, blue for suspicion, Red for threat. For two nights the skies above Kolog flickered with green.

Then one night Lunaara as part of a routine came to the coordinates of Silora. But to his shock, at the same coordinates now there were empty musical lands of Kolog.

As if Silora never existed.

She now noticed the harmony of Kolog's music had begun to detune not in a major way but in a very minute yet noticeable way.

Far from the vigilante trio, the true Astryn, drifted into solitude. They had chosen to Meditate in a city like no other. "**Aerealis**" resting on the coordinates 71.04 Degree a, 12.65 Degree F-A sacred city where fire froze instead of burned.

Aerealis was carved into a canyon of suspended flames-Each flame static, Hovering midair like petals caught in a timeless wind. The city didn't burn: It Glowed with cold warmth, paradoxically soothing. Buildings here were Formed of translucent fire blocks, their surfaces shifting between hues of Sapphire and crimson. Walls whispered ancient lullabies and streets crackled Underfoot like frozen lightning.

The air was dense with silence yet it sang. Meditation domes hovered like Inverted bells above pools of silver ash. The true Astryn entered one such dome, Light folding behind them. They sat, their form still as an unopened scroll, channeling their energy into the land beneath.

With every passing breath, the flames surrounding them glowed brighter. Aerealis responded. This city had always been connected to the core of Kolog, And with the Astryn now woven into it, their light intensified forming a Protective aura that subtly expanded outward. It was not a barrier of defense, but of amplification-The more they meditated the more their light intensified.

The Astryn's thoughts sank into the golden feet of Eldarion. But suddenly they Saw visions. Visions of their own light, visions of deception, visions of captured Cities, but these visions were not clear they were broken imagery. The Astryn Did not fight them, they let those visions pass redirecting their focus on their Breath.

The purpose was not the visions but to intensify their lights to create the light Prison, hence the meditation continued.

Lunaara thought she was lost the only possible answer to the question how can An entire city disappear overnight. So she changed her path still in search of Silora she descended to the coordinates 15.04 Degree East 77.29 degree kolog.

The city of **"Orellin".** Orellin was a city of bubbles, not just shaped from them But made of them. This is the most fragile city of Kolog. Each city, each Structure and soul formed of iridescent orbs.

Every time a bubble pulsed, it spoke. Conversations in Orellin were in the form Of bursts of misty color. The inhabitants- The **"Or'as"**Floated gently in and Out of buildings communicating through ripple and rhythmic popping. But each Burst meant death literally making it the most sensitive city of Planet Kolog. Children played with gravity, bouncing from bubble balconies to streets made Of gel foam.

Lunaara was mesmerized by Orellin however understanding the gravity of the Situation she moved to check the safety of the other cities. On her first pass, Lunaara had seen the city in full bloom-bubbles singing in crescendo, archways Made of airborne clusters, even schools floated like airborne jellyfish. But later That night when she visited the same coordinates again there was nothing.

No bubbles.

No hum.

No residue of burst life or even traces of collapse.

Empty detuned musical land.

It was as if Orellin never existed.

She tried to summon a green beam to signal peace but her claws wavered and The light flickered red. For the first time since her birth, panic colored her lights.

Far to the west, Nerion had wandered into a village few dared to light out aloud.-**"Moorae"** marked near coordinates-Kolog 11.88. A village carved not from stone Or Cloud, or Bubble or Jelly but from sensation itself. Here, emotion was Architecture. Reality responded to feeling. The air itself was laced with moods-Each breath a potion, each step a spell.

The ground of Moorae shimmered with what the locals called **"Moorstones"-** Crystalline fragments that changed hue and pulsed. With every step here Nerion Was someone else delighted, furious, nostalgic, and terrified. The stones didn't Judge they simply translated the unspoken. In Moorae your feet told secrets Your mouth never would.

But it wasn't only the stones. The very scent of the city bent the spirit. They Were streets that smelled like unspoken apologies, alleys that breathed old Romance, plazas filled with the scent of a mother's lullaby or the bitter ozone of Betrayal. The fragrances of Moorae weren't constant-They shifted with the wind, with your memories, with the state of your mind. The inhalation of an even A single breath could spiral a creature of Euphoria, grief, or awe.

The inhabitants-Called the **"Moors** "were not of flesh, but of living flicker. Each being was a delicate stream of scented flame and scented smoke, Flickering like candle light caught in a memory. They drifted like incense Across the streets, changing form with each passing emotion. No face, no limbs Just feeling, given color and fire.

The moors did not speak. They resonated. If you were joyful they curled around You in golden spirals. If you were lost, they shimmered purple and led the way. Communication here was not in words, but in empathic flame-A language that Burned into the soul.

On his second evening, while crossing **"The Velvet Causeway** "A bridge that Evoked longing with every step-Nerion paused mid breath, overcome by scent So familiar so powerful that it hollowed him out. The scent of a memory he Didn't knew he'd buried.

But by the next dawn, Moorae was gone.

No rubble, No trace, No sound.

Just silence. A silence heavy with unanswered longing.

Meanwhile on the coordinates where Orellin existed, Lunaara began scanning The terrain using her **"Aura Spectrum** "She cast layers of photonic patterns Over the now empty detuned musical land hoping the memory of the city would Be retrieved by light. Each hue she cast tried to pull fragments from what has Vanished.

She examined temporal ripples. A bubble's burst left a lingering scent of salt-Sweet resonance-But here there was nothing. She dropped to the ground, Pressed her palm to the soil, closed her eyes and shot out lights. These were not Her normal lights these were static electric ancient lights of Emerald, Ruby and Corals. A fain bubble returned like a child laughing underwater but this was not Enough.

She then opened her wings made of shimmering, translucent stardust and flew Upwards, summoned the memory of her first sight of Orellin and projected it Into a sphere. It pulsed blue and then blinked away. She couldn't even hold a Memory of it and that terrified her more than its disappearance.

And that's when she knew someone was erasing it not just destroying but Unwriting.

Here Nerion took a different approach he sat on the coordinates of the now Empty, detuned musical land of the village of Moorae and began the first Chanting the first sound of the universe- The sound he had once used to break The shadow pole. The empty space around him vibrated but no structure Returned.

He then summoned vapor from his own body, Trying to create a Moor but the Mist only fell flat. No response. Nerion now began to question his own Memory, his sanity. Did he really experience Moorae? Or was it just an Illusion Of a tired mind, A mind tired from all his travels.

So he began a ritual where he slowly lifted both hands and began to carve **"The Freeze Chant"** from ice into the open empty space ahead of him frost burst into His fingers like pale fire, coiling into ancient glyphs of ice- spiraling runes that Hummed in dead languages. One by one they etched themselves into the fabric Of space. Hovering into a circle around him. The final glyph-Shaped like a Spiraled dagger made of thick snow burned blue and with a whisper of cracking air, **"Frezza"** emerged.

A towering mirror of thick, rimed frost levitating before him. Its surface Shimmered like frozen glass. Yet nothing of Nerion's reflection appeared only Cold frost. Only waiting silence.

Nerion lifted his palm and with the movement of one finger across the icy air, He traced a question in ice language-Patterns of snow-like lines and curling Frost that melted as they formed.

"Did Moorea even exist?"

Frezza the cosmic archive pulsed and from its mirrored heart, a single shard of ice floated outward crystalline, cube like, glowing from within.

Inside; A still image. A city made of translucent towers, swaying like liquid Glass beneath a sapphire sky. Streets woven with frozen moorstones. The moors Frozen like paused images.

Nerion touched the shard and the memory melted open and the city came alive. Not a vision but a frozen movie, unfolding within the shard, complete in Soundless echoes and silver hued light.

There it was.

Moorea. Not a hallucination, not an imagination but real.

The shard flickered once more, and then crumbled into powder. Frezza stood Silent again. It had shown what was asked. It would not explain the vanishing For that was not its purpose.

Nerion was now in a mix of relief and panic. Relief as Moorea was real, Panicked as it had vanished on his watch. He then reverted the freeze chant and Returned Frezza to its cosmic mystery.

He now moved towards Eclipse Veil for he knew only the Eclipse Veil had Answers to his questions. But before moving he first shootout lights of red in the Skies. Signaling Lunaara and Puffin of the potential threat.

On his way to the Eclipse Veil Nerion sees not one but many cities he had seen And experienced before were no longer were they used to be. This realization Only made his steps speedier he felt his chest burn with rage. Nerion has always Been in love of his father, Eldarion. He has always been a crazy admirer of his Creations which made him what he were-The cosmic traveler and now this Magical, beautiful cities vanishing threatened creation once again. He started Thinking could it be Draakara? Could it be someone else? Lunaara perhaps. He had only known Lunaara shortly how can he trust her? The answers to all These questions lay with the Eclipse Veil alone.

Chapter 22: Return to the Eclipse Veil

Nerion arrived at the mouth of the Veil- A place of nostalgia. Not the one that Would sooth your soul but an eerie one. Before him stood the Eclipse Veil Unchanging ever present draped in rainbow hues, its colorful liquid ever pulsing But with authority. It has been eons since he last stood there.

He lowered his head in a deep, solemn bow. Not as surrender but as a traveler Greeting the gatekeeper of unseen knowledge. If there was one thing he had Learnt from eons of his travels is this. When you seek knowledge, you bow. So He let silence accompany the bow for silence sometimes bore the weight of Understanding and reverence.

Then came the first flickers.

By the show of his hands he shot a swirl of soft white pulses mixed with slanted Violet streaks, sharp blue flares along with jet black lights towards The veil making patterns of spirals and Starlight signals which then slowly Disappeared as if someone erasing them.

“Eclipse Veil, I seek answers cities of Kolog vanish into silence. Who threatens Creation again is it Drakaara? Is it Lunaara?

The veil did not respond.

Nerion waited, his frosty form standing still. Only the frost trails behind him Melting into shimmering dust. The silence grew louder. He watched the veil Closely not even the faintest shimmer. It remained still as if nothing blind to his Lights.

A lesser being might have turned back. But Nerion knew truth is never granted-It is to be earned. He took a step forward. The space thickened, he could feel the Veil resist. Still he pressed further. More patterns emerging from his hands. A Crescendo of seeking. A visible ache blooming across his body of translucent Ice. He repeated his light plea again, stronger this time.

The veil stirred.

A subtle shimmered danced across its colorful liquid surface forming an Iridescent pulse. It was not a glow, it was more like a breathing mirror trying to Remember the face it once saw. The communication began.

Waves of Gold shimmer and swirl in harmonies from the Eclipse Veil.

"Who approaches the veil?"

Nerion took a step back. He composed his light, softened the intensity and Re Shaped his spirals shooting out lights of blush blue, silver and white Which Curved and formed patterns of domes made of galaxies, star dusts, Universes.

"I am Nerion, the cosmic traveler"

The Veil shimmered in response, This time more focused. Patterns began to Flicker on its surface. Forming and reforming in complex loops.

"Truth comes with a sacrifice. Are you willing to sacrifice that what you hold Most dear?"

A confused Nerion now shot out streams after streams of constantly flickering, Blinking yellow lights towards the Veil.

"I don't understand"

In response the Veil shimmered forming ice white ripples on its surface which Then made patterns of a frozen symbol- A necklace- which then quickly melted Away in the liquid.

"Frostace"

Nerion froze.

Frostace? His hand moved reflexively towards his chest. The necklace lay there. Nestled in his frosty body-A loop of icy filigree so delicate that it seemed like a Frozen memory. For others it may seem insignificant. A trinket. But for him-It Was monumental.

The veil did not elaborate. It never begged. It demanded. And in return, it Promised only truth.

Nerion looked up slowly. The pulsing liquid of the Veil was unwavering. It Would not negotiate.

A flurry of fragmented memories rushed through Nerion. He didn't want this. Not this. Frostace was not merely a necklace. They say it's merely a relic of Frost but that is a lie told by those too fragile to face the truth. Frostace was Once a heart-Beating not with blood but with something older than magic, Something ancient than creation.

Light.

She was brighter than the brightest. Purer than the purest. She was not born of Any world. She was a world. His world. Nerion the cosmic traveler once Wanted to settle for good. And it was in her arms. And when she died-Not in Battle, not in blaze but in silence, while smiling-The universe paused for a Breath it never exhaled again. Her body faded. Her lights became ashes of the Dark but her heart-Her heart fell into Nerion's hands.

He, made of glacial patience. He who never spoke of pain. He only knew how To hold things without breaking them. And so he held her heart. For centuries. For centuries more until what was once warmth became silence encased in Divine frost of which he made a necklace and name it Frostace.

Frostace now rests on his chest not to protect but to remind of what once was Of what can never be again. **"Frostace is her heart. The heart of the only Woman Nerion ever loved. His only weakness yet his greatest strength"**

He stood still, the demand burning in his chest.

"Do you truly ask this is of me?" he thought not aloud but inwardly-a whisper For the veil to hear in silence. But it gave no sign of remorse.

Nerion turned away, looking out at the distant horizon where Kolog once sang With life, now detuned, cities vanishing. If knowledge was power then this truth Could protect what remained.

Still-Frostace?

He clenched the necklace, cold spreading across his palm. The more he Hesitates, The more cities lost. His lights now began to dim struggling to hold His form. He was being torn not by the veil but the decision

What was more precious? Long lost love? Or a chance to save Kolog? To save The love of other creatures of these vanished cities?

Nerion now moved forward towards the Eclipse Veil with frostace now in his Hands. The patterns from his body began to fade voluntarily as if mourning. The Act of surrender wasn't just physical. It was soul-deep. A disrobing of the self.

Frostace hovered in his hand catching the subtle glint of the Veil's reflection.

He whispered one last pattern shooting out soft jagged blues wrapped in silver Spirals which then burst into cocoon like patterns.

"Take care of her"

He extended frostace into the veil. As it touched the shimmering rainbow Colored liquid surface. Tears made of ice rolled from his eyes to his ever Shifting face landing into the Eclipse Veil. The necklace and his cold tears Disappeared within, no splash, and no sound-Only absorption.

There was stillness.

Then the surface lit up.

Glyphs and Spirals began to appear not messages but omens.

The Eclipse Veil responded with two distinct revelations. The first came Through patterns. A sequence that twisted into itself, broke apart and rejoined In natural symmetry. The surface of the Veil formed patterns of twisting glyphs. Shadowed knots, Mirrored loops.

"One of your own wears a face not theirs. Skin borrowed. Heart stolen."

This got Nerion thinking. Who could it be it?

Could it be Drakaara? Could it be Lunaara? But he didn't interrupt. The Veil Wasn't done. The surface rippled again but this time not in patterns but in Imagery.

A vision unfolded.

Liquid light transformed into a moving memory, playing like a silent movie on The surface of Eclipse Veil. It was Lunaara's birth. The first Lunaar eclipse of The universe. The divine ballet of light and darkness. And then the **"Moonstone** "fell.

A glimmering shard chipped off from the moon landing on the musical lands of Kolog. It did not land near Lunaara-But to the north. Where a clay city stood on Kolog. The cities walls shuddered as the stone sank into its core. The clay Cracked then fused, veined with silver.

The city forgotten by most now held the key to Lunaara's genesis.

The vision faded. The truth had a price and Nerion had paid it with tears and With Frostace.

However Nerion did not move, he stood there in silence, recalling the visual in His mind on loop trying to make sense of it. Seeds of doubt began creeping in His frosty little heart. Could the earlier clue by the Veil be about Lunaara? Could she be secretly helping Drakaara? Was the birth of Lunaara some kind of A divine plan by Eldarion?

There were too many questions but no answers. But his thoughts were Interrupted by sharp straight, continuous brighter than ever green lights. A Signal by the Astryns. Nerion noticed these lights were spread in all the Directions of Kolog. And that is when he understood Him, Lunaara and Puffin Were being summoned. So he started following the source of these lights.

Chapter 23: Reunion

Light surged through the upper edge of the sky, not as a flare but as slow Desperate summons. The true Astryn's call did not ripple-It carved. Nerion, Puffin, Lunaara and the other Astryn drifted towards the lights which rested at Aerealis which became their gathering point.

As soon as they gathered the True Astryn began. It entire diamond form now Flickered with densely packed sequences of layered pulses-An announcement With no ambiguity. Shooting out extremely bright lights of all colors which Then formed patterns of soft peaceful circles which then burst into a cage like Structure.

"My light has reached maximum capacity. I am confident. I now possess the Strength required to contribute to the forging of the light prison" No wavering Patterns. No fluctuations in glow. The declaration was complete.

Yet something felt off. Lunaara's light dimmed slightly. Puffin who usually is The goofiest of them, always spreading joy, happiness strangely seemed to be Lost in some kind of thoughts. Nerion's eyes focused on Lunaara but in ways of Suspicion, the other Astryn flickered slowly as if considering its own readiness.

The true Astryn turned to the other Astryn directly projecting extremely Bright Yellow and Orange lights forming patterns of triangles but made of Nebulaes Which then burst into soft circles.

"And you? Have your meditations brought you the same strengths?"

There was a delay-A pause that registered as half as a breath. Then came the Response from the other Astryn. Its colors were uneven-Bright whites diluted With fractured grey. The message was simple but conflicted.

"Ye, ye yes I am."

The true Astryn did not immediately reply. Instead .it cycled through slow, Intricate diagnostic flares-A silent analysis. The slightest fragment of suspicion Bloomed not enough to alarm but enough to log something was off. The light Wasn't just flawed, it was intentionally flawed. It carried no emotional Signature. This was unnatural.

The silence between the true Astryn and the other was filled with too Many mute lights. But the true Astryn allowed the answer to settle, not pursuing The tension instead it recalibrated its light and shifted it to resume neutrality.

The True Astryn's body then flickered in lights of yellow, gold and silver which Then burst into semi circles trying hard but not able to form complete circles as If intentional.

"The forging will require clarity, We begin only when the circle is whole, only When you have meditated enough"

The other Astryn responded with a flicker that could be mistaken for a nod. It Did not offer protest, nor did it retreat. The act of acceptance was too clean-like A rehearsed surrender.

The true Astryn now looked at Lunaara, Nerion and Puffin immediately Catching up on energy, very strange, disrupted energy. So it shout out a ball of Forged from collective lights of its own hurling towards Lunaara, Nerion and Puffin which then burst into patterns of rectangles which further burst in 3 intertwined spirals.

"What is it that bothers you guys?"

Lunaara did not respond immediately. Her light patterns curled inward, showing turbulence beneath. Not fear, not panic wild unpredictable light that flickered In every spectral shade but blue.

Puffin usually a fountain of cheerful pulses and quicksilver glow, had no ripple. His lightning bolts and thunders had frozen into a quiet, slow-turning spiral. Dull. Clouded. A silence not just in thunders but in essence.

Nerion whose light always moved in deliberate symmetry had altered. His inner Core pulsed faster which was unnatural for ice. His outer frost shifted to the Hues of suspicion, particularly directed towards Lunaara.

The true Astryn released an extremely stronger light-sequence of Pinks, Maroons and Red Forming weird giant amoeba like patterns which then made a Huge dark red bubble which in turn burst with a huge sound quash mid air.

"It is my command bare before me what you hide. QUICK."

In response something unthinkable happened.

Lunaara, Puffin and Nerion flared at the same moment. Not similar. Not Parallel. Identical.

Their lights became one unified beam-Same intensity, Same hue, and Same rhythm. An unnatural harmony formed without rehearsal.

"Their message came in exact unison: The cities of Kolog are vanishing."

The true Astryn froze.

It played back the signal by pulling it backwards midair rewinding it, looping it Multiple times. Triple checked the wavelength, the density, the edge the Curvature of each ripple. There were no deviations. Not a single pixel out of Place.

This kind of Unison was impossible without forced alignment. But there had Been no moments to align which meant-

They were all witnessing the same thing. At the same time. In the same way.

The true Astryn now shot out all colors of lights. But these lights were Constantly blinking, flickering. No patterns this time just blinking flickering Lights of all colors.

"Explain"

In response Puffin shootout huge electric blue bubble which then bust into thunderbolts which slowly made Patterns of circles which then made holographic visuals of weird, magical, Crazy cities of Kolog which then disappeared without a trace, as if they never Existed.

"We didn't mean to align. It just happened. We all saw the same. Cities of Kolog disappearing as if they never existed. One day we are in the cities and the Next day, there is nothing. Empty detuned musical lands."

The true Astryn turned towards Lunaara shooting out soft lights of silvers and Indigo's making patterns the same holographic patterns of Puffin but its lights Blinked a few times.

"I sense there is something more to it Lunaara, but what?"

In response Lunaara's Dark red, Grey and Copper colored lights spun outwards, Then dimmed. Then again, and steadier. Her answer was difficult to convey not Due to the lights but due to weight.

"While investigating the vanishing cities, I discovered remnants. Not ruins but Remnants."

The true Astryn in response shootout flickering copper lights in quick motion.

"Remnants? Of what kind?"

In response Lunaara shot out rainbow colored lights which then burst into Patterns of paint brushes which then burst into big empty rectangles similar to Canvases.

"Painting, they were not of Kolog's. They felt alive."

Puffin shifted beside her. His thunder pulses sharp expressing concern. Nerion Remained still, but his internal pulses increased again.

Lunaara then continued and from the same lights formed multiple circles which intertwined With each other which then made vortex like pattern.

"And when I touched one of them, I hear screams. Screams arising from pain, Pressured as if trapped in strokes."

The other Astryn pulsed faintly, then dimmed. It did not contribute. It watched.

The true Astryn was silent. Flickering lights of silver across its body in waves But in extra slow motion. It was thinking.

Lunaara's projection intensified. Her pattern was jagged now, not because she Was lying. She wasn't but because she was reliving.

The room pulsed with the silence. No lights. No patterns. No one contradicted. No one questioned. No one mocked.

It was Nerion who shifted next. His lights darkened slightly, but his other layers Glowed tight Crimson pulses.

"I was warned"

The true Astryn now turned completely towards him again flickering lights of Copper this time the speed of the flickering was slightly higher than earlier.

"By whom?"

Nerion shot out silver lights which intertwined and formed the pattern of Eclipse Veil which then burst into patterns of broken chains.

"By The Eclipse Veil. It warned me of deception. Of betrayal from within"

The true Astryn now shot out lights of Pink, Red and Magenta forming reverse Spirals.

"Do you suspect anyone?"

Nerion didn't respond directly. Instead he flared lights of electric blue which Then made patterns of rectangle resembling canvases.

"I assume the paintings will guide us"

The true Astryn in response shot out rainbow colored lights across all directions illuminating the otherwise pink skies. These rainbow colored lights then came together and burst Which made patterns of a compass.

"Then let light be our compass"

Lunaara, Nerion, and Puffin they all agreed.

The portal formed slowly. Purposefully.

The moment travel began, The other Astryn sent out pulses. Subtle ones. Suggestions laced with soft misalignments. Hints of alternate co-ordinates. Memories cloaked in fog.

Lunaara noticed incorrect vectors.

The true Astryn noted, lights sharp frequencies bleeding. Lights had become eroded as if The compass was confused. So it sucked up the lights from the Other Astryn and shot out straight lights like threads of brightest Greens and Oranges forming patterns of multiple "X" shapes forming holographic images Of Lunaara. It also deleted the portal.

"Do not confuse Lunaara. Follow her trail, Lunaara the portal will be forged by Your lights"

Without wasting a single breath, Lunaara shot out pink, and red lights opening Up a portal which directly led to the paintings.

The location unraveled in pulses. A ridge. A wall of light. There were two dark Pitch Black canvases lying on the empty detuned lands of Kolog. The painting Had black lines. Lines that curled like tendons. Shadows that didn't follow Logic. Eyes that blinked without movement.

The silence was not empty. It watched.

The group circled the first mural. Its surface hummed and behind it. In the Patterns of paint. Something moved. The paintings flickered as if seeking help. They screamed.

Chapter 24: Shadow Beneath Light

The true Astryn remembered this place was once filled with creation, Light, Magic, carnivals but now it has become an empty detuned land. For the first Time in eons Kolog felt sick. Kolog needed to be cured. The two jets black Canvases before them contained two of the most happiest cities of Kolog. The Once vibrant lanes of these cities were now reduced to mere images, trapped in Paint. But it wasn't just the stillness of the scene that struck them: It was the Overwhelming sense of anguish emanating from the paintings.

The creatures within the paintings screamed, their mouths open in eternal pleas For help. Their eyes were wide with terror, their faces frozen in anguish as if Their very souls were caught in the act of reaching out. The brush strokes vivid And sharp seemed to pulse with their pain, as if images themselves were alive, Trembling with the force of their suffering. Lunaara's chest tightened as she felt The weight of despair that filled with air. Each scream dug into her heart like a Splinter that refused to be removed.

Puffin, his face pale and his eyes wide, could barely look at the scenes. The Lives trapped in these paintings were not strangers, some of them had been Friends being he had known for a quite a while now but now they were nothing More than tortured souls, their cries a silent testament to the horrors that had befallen them. His hand reached out, but he couldn't bring he couldn't bring Himself to touch the painted surface. The energy here was wrong, too Dangerous. And yet, he couldn't't' tear his gaze away from the faces, each one Crying out for salvation, each one begging for release.

Nerion's hands raised as if he wanted to communicate something but his lights Failed him. This wasn't something he had ever imagined. He had heard of Drakaara's painting but seeing them live terrified him. He felt a sudden Coldness spread within him, something that didn't come from within him but From the paintings.

The true Astryn's form flickered with a pulse of light. Its body shimmering as It observed the paintings. There was no visible reaction of distress on its Triangular face, yet ripples in its lights were unmistakable. It was sensing the Same agony. Even the Astryn could not remain indifferent to the suffering Trapped within these paintings. A deep hum resonated from within as if the Very fabric of its heart was being ripped apart.

Finally it shot out lights of Dark Red and Crimson which then slowly turned Into pitch black lights which made patterns of spider webs made of jet black Strings.

"These are the doings of Drakaara"

The lights around it flickered, as if to emphasize the gravity of the light and Patterns. It paused before flickering, blinking the same colored lights in Urgency and this time the Red, Crimson and Jet black lights intertwined To make patterns of complex bubbles resembling shields.

"But how? How could she infiltrate Kolog when all of you were on guard?"

There was no answer only the empty detuned lands.

Seeing this pulse became erratic, a flash of red flickering within its spectrum Making patterns of red thunderbolts.

"Answer Me"

Very rarely do the Astryn's get angry and this was one of those moments. The Question of how Drakaara had managed such a feat was one that gnawed at Everyone present. How had she slipped past the defenses of Puffin, Nerion, and Lunaara? How did she breach their watchful eyes and imprisoned the cities in This manner? And what was alarming was there was no warning, Not even the Slightest indication of a breach. The defenses were strong, their vigilance Unbroken. Then how did she manage to pull such a feat?

The true Astryn's crystalline form flickered again, a brie flash of light betraying Its frustration. It turned it gaze towards Nerion whose eyes narrowed in Thoughts. The true Astryn seemed to sense the connection between Nerion's Previous warning and the situation at hand. As its light shifted, it cast a fleeting Glance at the other members of the group, searching for some answers in their Faces.

The true Astryn's light patterns began to ripples in waves, A quiet hum of Thought. The others watched in silence, waiting. The true Astryn now began Suspecting everyone. Nerion's warnings of betrayal were playing in her mind on Loop. A surge of light seemed to pulse from the true Astryn, wrapping around The group like an invisible wave. The energy was unsettling, the hum sharp And piercing as the Astryn's mind pieced the fragments together. A series of Fractured patterns flashed in its awareness-Broken lights, faint glimmers of Something dark that had entered the fold. The Astryn's pulse grew stronger, The colors becoming more intense as it made the connection. Nerion had Warned them of betrayal, of cracks in the unity of their own kind. He noticed How the other Astryn's light earlier had been tainted, With black lights. Black Lights were foreign to the Astryns. How the other Astryn tried to confuse Lunaara when she was forging the portal to here.

Nerion's mind raced, the fragments of information falling into place like pieces Of puzzle he had long ignored. He had known something was wrong. He had Felt the shift in the air when the Astryn's light had begun to flicker, their Patterns corrupted by an unknown presence. They had been whispers, faint Echoes of something very wrong but he hadn't understood now standing Before the paintings, things were beginning to add up.

Nerion's gaze sharpened as the realization hit him. The fracturing of the lights had started long before their arrival here. Drakaara's influence had been subtle. Creeping into their midst, Weaving her presence into the very fabric of the Communication. The cracks in the other Astryn's lights were not random. They Were signals. Signals of Deception. The corruption had spread, twisting the Unity of the Astryn's from within.

The true Astryn now shot out wild flickering lights of Violet, Indigo and Blue Which made patterns like ocean waves which then intertwined to Form sound waves which then burst into patterns Of the Shadow Pole which later burst into stars, galaxies, Asteroids, Meteors.

"But why? Is it revenge? Revenge for Lunaara snatching away the Shadow Pole And getting it here? Or for Nerion as he broke the

Shadow Pole restoring the Universe using the first chant of the universe?"

This question made Nerion's thoughts turn inward, recalling the vision from The Eclipse Veil-The sight of the moonstone falling from the moon on the night Of Lunaara's birth. The vision had shown him more than just the fall of the Moonstone. He hadn't fully understood the significance of it then hence he had To share the information with the others.

So Nerion with the show of his hands shot out a pulse of frozen light through The air. A series of series of sharp clear patterns began to form making thick ice In mid air on which he played the information about the moonstone like a movie On a projector. The stone chipped off from the moon had been no coincidence. It was a part of something larger. The energy from the Moon stone sparked Something deeper.

Nerion's light patterns began to weave a more complex narrative as the visuals Kept playing explaining the stone falling from the moon right at the moment of Lunaara's birth. As the information washed over them, The true Astryn's light Shimmered within its body in circular waves. A mark of recognition. The true Astryn now remembered the stone but Lunaara caught More of their attention than the stone. Hence all the Astryn's apart from the spy Astryn concentrated on the Moon Stone. However the spy Astryn from earlier Focused on the moonstone. The spy Astryn immediately sensed what it is. This Was the same Astryn that had manipulated the other Astryn's to believe Lunaara was a threat. The pieces were aligning now, and the truth was clear as ice. One of the cities Called **"Cavalium-The city made of Clay"** had sucked up the moonstone. Drakaara was trapping the Cities of Kolog in search of the Moonstone. But this revelation also forged new Questions. Why the moonstone? What is the Moonstone? Does it have to do Something with Lunaara? How will the moon stone aid Drakaara?

The true Astryn's pulse flickered, its light pulsing with a new urgency. It turned Towards the others, its pattern sharp and insistent.

"Now we confront her"

The confrontation had come and now there was no turning back. The true Astryn though still uncertain of Drakaara full motives knew that they could no Longer delay the inevitable. Many cities of Kolog have already been trapped by Drakaara. The light around it shimmered with a powerful, commanding energy And its pulse quickened as it turned to face the other Astryn-The one who had Been betraying them.

The true Astryn's shot out wild flickering lights of bright Gold and silver and Hurled it towards the other Astryn. These lights landed on its feet and started Making loops thereby trapping the Astryn in its place. It then shot out extremely Bright lights of Velvet, Crimson and Scarlet making patterns of black balls Which expanded into patterns of eyes.

"Since when are you too serving Drakaara as a spy?"

The other Astryn's lights flickered through its body nervously, its patterns Trembling as if unsure how to respond. Its lights now had a darkening hue to its Glow. The true Astryn had noticed it earlier and now with truth about the Moonstone learned the true Astryn was sure the other Astryn was also turned Rogue but it wanted to know since when?.

The other Astryn now shot out lights of dark Green, making patterns of Circles Which then formed patterns of a smile through its mouth since its Hands and Legs were trapped by the gold and silver loops shot out by the True Astryn.

"I am not your enemy, I am innocent"

But the True Astryn was not convinced. The pressure from the Gold and Silver Loops grew more intense. The True Astryn then shootout a storm of bright lights of Blue, Yellow, Pink, Orange, and Green and made it swirl around them like a Tornado. While hurling thunderbolts after thunderbolts in a succession of 5 on It.

"Reveal the shadow beneath the light, show us what you are hiding. The Universe demands Truth"

The other Astryn's light began to falter, the intensity wavering, Until Finally the Truth was revealed. A pulse of dark energy exploded from within the other Astryn and in an instant its true form was revealed.

Drakaara stood before them, her shape now fully revealed. A sinister smile on Her face, holding the nullweave in her hand like the spin of an enemy raising it In the sky as her greatest achievement leaving everyone in shock.

The true Astryn understood that the real other true astryn was trapped in that Dark, evil canvas. However it refused to believe that even the kids of God. Even The kids of Eldarion could also be trapped in the dark canvases of Drakaara.

So it shot out extremely wild nonstop flickering lights of dark red and velvet Making random unreadable patterns.

"This, this is impossible"

Drakaara then responded by shooting out thick waves of jet black lights forming Patterns of Infinity.

"Darkness is an ocean of unlimited possibilities"

Chapter 25: The Moonstone

The Astryn shot out lights of pale yellows, and oranges making rapid patterns of canvases which then burst into patterns resembling a reverse octopus?

"How, how did you conjure a canvas that dark? A canvas which has the Ability to devour even us?"

From across the abyss. Drakaara shot out 2 thin lines of dark lights from the Show of her hand which then began to dance forming complex cobwebs of Darkness which then burst into two big white and black balls resembling the Moon, These balls then erupted into galaxies, universes, stars like a fountain Making weird figures and shapes almost human but not humans, the patterns Ended with forming a bony structure which then melted into dust.

"While you danced with your precious moon-born beast, breaking the shadow Poles, Searching Nerion, I searched downward. I floated to another universe. A Universe of lesser frequency, A universe where light existed but only in parts. A Universe where gods were beings of immense power but poor things didn't Know their potential so I simply captured them in my paintings and from the Bones of the most powerful of them I made this my masterpiece, my most Precious canvas. A canvas that can even capture the Astryns"

This revelation spread a shockwave among all of them. Making them freeze. They were left lightless. Very rarely do the Astryn's were out of lights and this Was one of such moments.

Nerion now with the show of his hands shot out rhythmic waves of ice white And blue making patterns of two hands which came across and joined in the form of Prayers towards Lunaara.

"I am sorry Lunaara"

Lunaara then responded with sending flickering green and orange lights Towards him in confusion.

"But why?"

Nerion then responded by sending frozen white, indigo and pink lights forming Cup like semi circles towards her.

"Because I was doubting you. Considering you as the traitor"

Lunaara then responded with shooting out lights of Bright yellow, purple, and indigo And red which then formed patterns of intertwined Hexagons.

"Its nothing new, so I forgive you."

Nerion's suspicion did not bother her. There was something else which was Bothering her. So Lunaara then took a step forward, its lights trembling but Resolute.

She then shot out lights of shimmering gold, velvet , silver and magenta towards Drakaara forming balls of electricity which eroded into tiny shockwave, the Shockwave then made holographic images resembling trapped cities of Kolog But these holographic cities were not still, they were distorted like a glitch.

"But if you possess such immense powers why bother tiny cities of Kolog?"

Drakaara's responded by shooting out thick jet black lights but smooth as silk Which made patterns of dark orbs which burst into semi circles floating in air. Which then formed patterns resembling open books towards Lunaara?

"I acted on the sequence once pulsed to me by the Astryn. The spy. My friend. That night its lights could not hide your truth. A truth neither of the other two Astryn had sensed."

Lunaara in response shout out thick rapidly pulsating lights of yellow and Orange towards Drakaara making random unreadable patterns.

"I, I do not understand. Explain"

Drakaara then responded by shooting out thick silver and black lights Forming Pattern of moon. But this moon had a slight crack on it. It then Sent out another Wave of same silver and black lights

but this time these Lights formed patterns of an eclipse towards Lunaara.

"On the night of your birth, there was something else that happened. Something so tiny that it missed the Astryn's eyes however my friend. The Spy Astryn noticed it. A stone from the moon fell on **Cavallium**. And Cavallium sucked it Its core."

Lunaara then responded with by shooting out Dark, Crimson, Velvet and Maroon Light waves which then formed a pattern of the cracked moon which then Formed pattern of huge star which was filled with Constantly moving spirals.

"But why is this moon stone so important to you?"

To which Drakaara then responded by sending out thick jet black light Waves as a thick as a blanket towards Lunaara which then made patterns Of a huge coiled Serpent when then melted like dust

"Because that stone is the only source of your powers, I destroy it, I destroy You"

Lunaara smirked then responded by shooting dark red lights towards Drakaara which then got compressed into orbs which started bouncing on The detuned lands of Kolog(In mockery)

"So have you found the moonstone? Have you found Cavallium"

The Astryn now interrupted shooting out lights of twisted Greens, Blues and Gold towards Lunaara which made patterns of complex spirals inside spirals The movement of every spiral differed from the other.

"Cavallium is not easy to locate Lunaara. Its co-ordinates are ever shifting. Cavallium was the first city of Kolog."

Cavalium is not a city in the usual sense, The Astryn;s light continued. It's a City of mystic clay and ancient rhythms. The material of its foundation flows, Breathes in unfathomable ways. The Astryn's patterns glowed brighter as if Pulling the memory of cavallium from the moment Kolog was created . It is a city where memory and dust

Converge, where the mist coalesces into shape. It is a city that resisted the very Concept of fixed coordinates.

Cavallium is home to the **"Cavali"-** Beings made of smoky clay. They appear As wavery outlines, like heat shimmer, but when upon closer inspection, their Forms resemble structures crafted from smoky clay, suspended mid-air. Their Bodies are fractured silhouettes, always shifting filled with moving runes that Pulse and flow like waves in a storm. Each Cavali seems both present and absent An apparition that bends the air around it, casting fleeting shadows that vanish Before they settle. They have no faces, no fixed form only a shifting mass of Warmth, smoke and clay, their presence felt in the very atmosphere of Cavallium.

The magic of the Cavali is as fluid and ever-changing as their bodies, They do Not weave spells in the traditional sense. Instead they shape the very essence of Their clay and smoke, manipulating the world around them through will alone. With a mere thought they moves pieces of their clay bodies into weapons, Shields or tools, only to see them dissolve into smoke seconds later, leaving behind nothing but a whisper of heat. Their magic is tactile-Clay is shaped, Fractured and reformed with the smoke they release bends reality, warping Space and matter for brief moments. Each act of creation pulls from their core And without careful control, the cavali risk losing their form entirely, fading into The smoke from which they were born.

The silence that followed weighed heavy as though the weight of the revelations Hung in the air. Lunaara, Nerion and Puffin's light dimmed for a moment. Their Light shifted moving with a delicate grace, their eyes tracing the unseen lights Of a cosmic truth.

As they were understanding the moonstone. Drakaara was back to her sinister Ways. The air around them suddenly grew thick, crackling with an energy which Did not belong to Kolog, it was foreign. The air suddenly was filled with thick Black lines followed by intensely dense fog. The ritual had begun.

Drakaara still holding the Nullweave, the prison to the Astryn now let it suspend In mid air while she extended her hands, Palms open, Eyes closed chanted an Undecodable ancient whisper and in a jiffy closed her palm as if squeezing Something. The Astryn understood that she was trying to drain the power of the Trapped Astryn.

So the Astryn who was tried to attack Drakaara but her attack couldn't even Touch her as if an invisible force field was protecting her. But this was not it. Lunaara sensed that something sinister. Drakaara was not just sucking up the Astryn's power but she was merging with it. Becoming it.

Drakaara's fingers twitched and the once brilliant glow of the Astryn's light Began to fade, flickering out like dying stars. Their power, their wisdom, their Very essence, was being siphoned away-Absorbed into the void of the Nullweave. The light that once emanated from the Astryn's fell silent, Swallowed by the darkness she had created.

The nullweave shimmered, its edges curling like smoke as the trapped Astryn Form disintegrated into fleeting sparks of light. Its lights were silenced, erased From existence, its flickering essence now nothing more than a ghost in the vast Emptiness of the fabric she had woven. The ritual was complete.

Drakaara's body pulsed with newfound energy, the duality of her being was Manifesting in ways that defied understanding. Drakaara had sucked up all Light, energy and magic of the trapped Astryn. Her body now began to flicker In thick blankets of light and dark, creation and destruction. She had become Both yet she was neither. Her essence had now become a combination of Opposites.

Her eyes glowed with the intensity of a thousand suns, while shadows swirled Around her darkening the space she occupied. Her skin shimmered between the Pale glow of starlight and the deep abyss of night, A physical manifestation of The forces she now controlled.

Drakaara's lips curled into an evil smirk. She had crossed the threshold. She Was no longer the creature who had walked this path in search of power. She was the power itself, a force that would reshape everything in her own image. There would be no turning back now.

As the energy settled, Drakaara took a step forward, her movement graceful yet Unsettling. The Nullweave once a barrier, now parted before her as if bowing to Its new master. The darkness that had once surrounded her seemed to gather, Swirling like a vortex, drawn to her in reverence, she has now become the Embodiment of both light and darkness-Two opposite forces bound together in A chaotic, unyielding unity.

Her pulse, once erratic and uncertain, now beat with the steady rhythm of a Conqueror. Now the moonstone, her ultimate goal appeared to be closer than Ever before.

But in the back of her mind, a flicker of doubt lingered. The moonstone with all Its power would not bend to her will as she had hoped. It was not an object Which could be claimed. It was a force that would demand more of her than she Could possibly anticipate. It could not even be located let alone be controlled.

But that thought was fleeting, drowned beneath the wave of power that surged Through her. She had come this far and now there would be no turning back.

The Astryn stood still in the center of the clearing, eyes fixed on the place where The Nullweave once was inside which was the trapped Astryn, no longer Trapped, no longer helpless just gone. Dead. What Drakaara had consumed was Not just light and magic but an entire piece of divinity. The Astryn's form Began to pulse in random multiple lights of grief, rage and revenge.

She raised both hands, palms open to the sky, and began the ritual in silence. A Slow wave of violet light rippled outward from her core, drawing a perfect Circle around her and the others. Nerion stepped into it first, his head lowered, His hands bare. Lunaara followed, letting motes of golden breath spill from her Fingers, drifting upward like floating embers. Puffin took his place last. His Other wise smiling face was sad now. The air around them softened-As if it was Mourning too.

The Astryn then shot out ultra slow pulse of deep blue but this time it was Radiated directly through her chest then faded into silver. The meaning was Clear. She is returned. Not lost, not erased. Returned-To the source-To Eldarion.

In response Lunaara extended one hand and shot out slow lines of copper Which did not make any patterns this time they just danced briefly before Unraveling. Offering her sacred gesture to honor the dead.

Puffin let out a single glittering shard into the pink sky above which upon Touching the sky burst into tiny pieces of shard resembling a firecracker.

Nerion closed his eyes uttering holy chants and then with the show of his hands He made an ice sculpture in memory of the dead Astryn. But this was not an Ordinary sculpture. It was alive. It could see, it could move. A perfect frosty Replacement for the Astryn.

Around them the world did not move. No wind, no flame, no breath of stars. Only presence. They stood in silence. They then in unity, in chorus formed out Extremely bright white lights into the pink skies to form patterns of Triangle Inside a triangle.

This meant "Return to the pattern". A version of rest in peace.

Once the ritual was completed. Astryn, Lunaara, Nerion and Puffin were in for Another shock. As they turned around expecting to face Drakaara, they were Greeted with another Astryn. The traitor. The one who was earlier sent to Hell. But there was something different about. Its entire form was now made of pitch Black diamonds. A literal dark Astryn.

This only made the other Astryn furious. And so in response it shot out sharp Lights of electric red and orange flaming hieroglyphs.

This meant **"ACT OF WAR"**

Chapter 26: Act Of War

In response to this Drakaara screamed not in fury but in rhythm. The war drums Of darkness echoed from her throat, ancient and guttural. Each pulse struck the Pink skies like a forgotten curse remembered. Each vibration twisted the fabric Of Kolog's breath.

And from these shattered sound waves came the first monsters- **The Shadow howlers.** They didn't walk, the unfurled. Black wolves stitched from Smoke and ashes, eyes hallow, ribs visible through mist, their howls curving the Air like blankets.

They circled Drakaara in rhythm, as if the scream was still dancing through Them. The dark Astryn was now gleaming with the powers of darkness granted To them by Drakaara. Its pitch black diamond skin, runes writhing in spirals, Not lines. Its body shimmered like frozen oil under a dead star. Its presence bent The light around it.

Drakaara now raised one jagged

arm and slammed it into the soil from the Impact zone crawled the **Inkborn Titans,** Giants of ink and bone dust, ten Stories tall and dissolving at their edges like cursed paintings.

The army of darkness now stood complete.

Drakaara, The Dark Astryn, Shadowhowlers, and Inkborn Titans were all ready To Face the army of Light.

Lunaara's skin rippled with starlight, Her expressions unreadable. Her energy Was carved in stillness.

At her side stood the Astryn, its form began radiating extremely dark red lights Rising slowly from its skin like flames. Its eyes sharper now fixated towards the Dark Astryn consumed by anger and disgust. The betrayal from the Dark Astryn still stung hard.

Puffin began to get scared and hence as a reflex action its body began to float a Few centimeters above the musical lands. His mouth for once was shut. His Lights began to grow feeble.

Nerion stepped forward, rhythmic, deliberate, ice blooming beneath each step Like music taking form and behind him walked the living ice sculpture of the Dead Astryn. Its crystalline arms etched with runes that hummed frost-tone into The wind. This was the army of light.

Two forces, one universe and in between them stood silence. Not the haunting One but the soothing one. A silence which stood as a testimony to peace before War.

The dark Astryn moved first.

Its jagged arm rose again, ruined in spirals of obsidian hate, and slammed it Across the Astryn standing beside Lunaara. The blow struck like judgment Tearing through the Astryn's radiant diamond form. A deep scar tore through it Marking without doubt the beginning of War.

In response with the show of its hands shot Event Horizon Orbs in the hopes of Killing the dark astryn once and for all.

But the dark astryn didn't dodge instead it opened its arms and the orbs sank Into its chest like pearls slipping into black water. It consumed them. Swallowed them whole. Each orb vanished with a muted hum, as if it were not Destruction but a delicacy.

The battle field stood stunned.

The Astryn, Puffin, Nerion and Lunaara were stilled. They had never seen Anything like this before. Seeing their reaction the dark astryn now passed a Grin as evil as the devil himself.

What once used to be the sanctuary of the Astryn's had now become battlefield. Sensing this Kolog's music land changed their melody to that of deep sad and Sorrowful. From the side of Drakaara, the InkBorn Titans extended their Massive dripping arms without taking a single step and launched arc of **Ink Erosion-** Black, steaming beams of acidic ink that upon touching would peel its Opponent's flesh aimed at the forces of light.

From Lunaara's side, Nerion took a step forward then raised both arms and Slammed them down in Rhythm. A rolling **Cryo Pulse-** Burst from the Sorrowful land beneath him spreading outwards like a frozen shockwave. The Ink beams met the cryo wave midair- and shattered into a storm of steam and Shards evaporating before they could even land.

In the shadows above, a shadowhowler let loose its power. Its throat stretched Unnaturally wide and form its jaw erupted a sharp, spiraling **Sound Surge Bite.** A compressed sonic projectile racing towards the Astryn like an invisible blade.

The Astryn didn't move. Its body flickered once-Then fired a sudden wide Entropy Surge. The chaotic wave met the sonic bite head-on. The collision Warped the air into glass like fractals before both powers dissolved into violet Dust.

Drakaara lifted her left hand and folded darkness in her palm like a blooming Flower with a flick she hurled three shrieking **Wail Bombs-** Crackling spheres Of Compressed spectral force shot directly towards Lunaara.

Lunaara responded in silence. She inhaled slowly, then exhaled her devastating Eclipse Breath. The violet-Black beam lance through the air colliding with the Wail bombs mid-flight all three exploded early, dissolving into writhing shadow And smoke before they could reach her.

At her side, the Astryn turned its gaze to the titans raising both its arms it Summoned the void nexus mid-air. The fabric of space tore open and faceless, Shifting voidspawn launched outwards like spears, their bodies slamming into Titan beams and unraveling into light upon contact.

One of the inkborn titans retaliated raising both massive arms and slamming Together. A distant **Weight Shatter** ripple expanded outward- A wave of raw Pressure that cracked the ground beneath everyone's feet but never touched Skin.

Nerion responded immediately his palms opened and from them shot a barrage Of whistling **Icicle Barrage** shards, twisting in the sir like crystalline missiles. They struck the ripple mid flight, freezing the shockwave into a fractured dome That exploded in frosted silence.

And then puffin rose.

He spun in mid air, arms flared out like a dancer and from his fingertips rained Shimmering energy rings each one bouncing from one titan to another bursting Just close enough to blind, never to bruise.

Lunaara hovered higher she summoned a plasma bomb held it at her chest for a Moment then hurled it with finality. The plasma bomb struck true. Its golden Blue explosion swallowed one of the inkborn titans whole and when the light Cleared, nothing remained of its towering form but smoking bone shards and Hissing black ink.

The army of darkness had taken it first wound. Now only two inkborn titans, four shadowhowlers, the dark astryn and Drakaara remained.

Across the field, the army of light stood unbroken. Not a single soul lost. Not Yet.

In retaliation the two remaining inkborn titans raised their arms in eerie Synchrony. They launched twin beams of ink erosion- Black, boiling energy Slicing through the air like horizontal blades. The beams hissed, burning away Even the glow left behind by past spells.

The Astryn reacted instantly, its chest flared and it released Solar Echo- Three successive waves of burning light. The first two waves met the titan's Beams mid air neutralizing them in a radiant explosion. The third beam pierced Through striking one titan in the side and sending a chunk of dripping obsidian Splattering into the void.

From behind them Drakaara stepped forward calm and deliberate. She raised Her hand and conjured a row of **Wail Bombs.** Each spinning with shrieking Energy they cut through the air like cursed artillery and aimed it straight Towards Lunaara.

Lunaara unshake exhaled sharply a sweeping arc of Eclipse Breath but this time With higher intensity erasing the bombs mid flight in a wave of black violet Annihilation. No debris remained- only silence.

Without pause she shot out another plasma bomb but this one was charged with Far greater force. She hurled it at Drakaara, a direct strike meant to pierce the Heart of darkness but before it could land, two shadowhowlers surged forward Forming a shifting wall of smoke and fang. The bomb exploded against them Instead. Sending the beasts reeling but sparing Drakaara barely.

The battlefield pulsed with exhaustion and fury. Magic no longer danced, it Collided. Every spell flung now had purpose. Every blast was meant to end Someone.

The last remaining inkborn titan raised its towering arms and with one Thunderous motion, it slammed together, releasing a violent Weight Shatter Wave.

A pressure quake of energy rippling across the field, targeted straight at the Heart of the Nerion. But it wasn't Nerion who stood to face it.

It was the living ice sculpture.

It lifted both crystal arms and summoned a wall of refracting frost. The Shockwave stuck the wall and shattered breaking apart in spray of harmless Vapor.

The sculpture then struck back from its palm launched two precise bolts of Frozen air, cutting clean through one of the titan's breaking its limbs chunks of Black ink sprayed streaming as they landed.

The shadowhowler last of its kind, howled from the sideline. It launched a Spiraling sound surge bite towards the sculpture.

The ice being spun once, projected a temporary ice dome mid air and the sonic Slammed into it, echoing around before dissolving harmlessly.

From above Drakaara raised her hand with surgical precision, she painted five Glyph-like slashes through the sky not art but co-ordinates and from them she Hurled three shrieking Wail Bombs and two vicious **Ghoul Morphs** directly at the structure.

The living ice sculpture turned. From its chest, a burst of frost sprayed upwards, Freezing one Ghoul Morph into shards mid flight. It then raised its arm and Launched another glacial javelin intercepting a Wail Bomb which detonated Into harmless smoke.

But the next wave was faster, stronger.

The second ghoul morph pierced through its left shoulder. A burst of acidic Black shadow exploding across its structure and before it could respond the last Wail bomb struck center mass.

And bomb the explosion swallowed it.

When the smoke cleared nothing stood in its place. Only shattered crystal, half Melted ice and silence. The light side had taken its first causality. The ice Sculpture was gone.

For a moment, the battlefield was still. The shattered remains of the ice Sculpture glistened like a broken prayer. And then everything erupted.

The final inkborn titan roared without voice and released a massive ink erosion Wave from its chest. It tore across the field in a black curtain, melting air, stone And spell residue in its path.

The Astryn stood stall and fired a diagonal **Prism Cleave,** A slash of Crystallized starlight that cut through the ink wave splitting it into twin arcs that Veered harmlessly off course.

At its side Nerion launched into motion. He extended his arms skyward and From the clouds above, he summoned a downpour of frozen spikes. They rained In unison. His Icicle Barrage targeting the titan's chest whose limb was already Broken earlier. Four shards struck, bursting on impact in cold shockwaves Which later exploded.

A frustrated, enraged Drakaara now responded with violence, she spun, hair Whipping around her like a second shadow, and painted the air with five dark Strokes. Each stroke gave birth to a new ghoul morph shot towards Nerion, Hissing and screaming.

He raised a quick glacier guard the wall forming just at the precise moment to Block them, the ghouls exploded in flame and smoke against its icy surface.

Lunaara now hovered in mid air, her eyes glowing brighter than stars she now Exhaled a vast eclipse breath , a wide horizontal blast that swept across the sky Like a blade of the void. It clashed against the Dark Astryn.

Dark Astryn countered with a **Gravity Pulse.** Slamming its palm together. The Impact twisted at the beam upward, deflecting it into the sky where it burst Harmlessly into black light.

Lunaara spun mid air and summoned a Plasma Bomb charged with a flick of her Wrist, and hurled it downwards at the last shadowhowler. The bomb exploded Mid-fall catching the creature in the in the blast when the smoke faded, only One leg remained.

The only remnants of darkness were Drakaara, Dark Astryn and one serving Ghoul Morph still circling the battlefield like a satellite.

A still floating Puffin raised his arm again. A ring of colored energy spiraled Around him, this time tighter, denser, more focused. He flung it like a blade of Joy into the sky, and it exploded above the ghoulmorph not enough to kill but Enough to knock it backwards in a storm of scattered limbs.

The Astryn raised both hands together. A brilliant Entropy Surge followed Crackling the musical terrain and forcing Drakaara and his minions to shift Backward, her coat of shadows fraying as the wave rushed past.

Lunaara now one with momentum activated the **Veil Reversal-** Splitting into Three bodies mid air. One silver, one black and one ash white. They each raised A hand and launched beams of tightly woven starlight straight towards the Ghoulmorphs body.

The blast struck hard. The ghoulmorph spun out limbs searing but still alive Barely. It retreated into the shadows behind the Dark Astryn, its form now Limping, its scream no longer stable.

All around them, the sorrowful musical land of Kolog was becoming the face of Destruction, with ashes and flames decorating the battlefield, the echoes of the Fallen titans, Ice sculpture and burned illusions still hung above.

Only 2 figures stood in the army of darkness now. Two who had the might of Thousands. Drakaara and Dark Astryn were both fuming engulfed in Anger, Rage. They needed revenge for their fallen commorades. The battlefield was not Past the game of numbers. It was about honor and sacrifice.

The winds stopped. The battleground was becoming a graveyard. No more Movement, no more thunder only final positions and those brave enough to step Into them.

Nerion did. He moved forward alone, unshaken his breath turning the silence Colder. His shoulders carrier not just ice but the quiet knowing of farewell.

Drakaara stood still. Unblinking, unreadable. The dark astryn beside her pulsed Like a diamond shaped heart, black, immersive, unreadable.

Lunaara, Puffin, Astryn watched him. No one tried to stop him because sometimes some exists belonged only to the one who chose them.

Nerion raise his arms. Frost licked up his forearms like a prayer undone above Him the sky cracked open. A blizzard of **Cryo Pulse** surged from the heavens, Spiraling downward in a wide dome freezing the battlefield mid air, locking the Edges of darkness in a temporary prison.

Drakaara staggered. The Dark Astryn's limb froze in place, if only for a second.

Astryn turned and fired an Entropy Surge into the freezing vortex this Shockwave of chaos that shattered the ground.

Lunaara soared overheard her hair ablaze with light and cut the sky with a Straight edged Eclipse Breath piercing the dark astryn's shoulder causing a Deep scar on it.

Still Nerion did not stop.

He raised both hands to the cloud again and summoned another Icicle Barrage Not scattered this time but one concentrated line of destruction aimed straight For Drakaara.

The ice fell like punishment.

She disappeared under it. For a moment, just for a moment. It looked liked the Storm had claimed her. But then from within the mountain of frozen wraith, a Shadow moved and stepped out.

Drakaara, her robes torn, her cheeks cut, her eyes unchanged. She blinked once And then Nightmare Induction cast this time not with arms but with intent. A Thin black thread of shadow slipped from her gaze. It lanced across the field, Curving, hissing, diving and pierced Nerion's skull with surgical stillness. And In that moment he saw her, The love of his life so he chose love over war. Nerion did stopped , his eyes began to gleam with Happiness, For the first time In eons he felt alive. But what he failed to understand was that this was just an Illusion. Before Astryn could warn him. His skull was ripped open by one of the Tendrils shot at his skull by Drakaara's left hand killing him in an instance. He Dropped like a mountain breaking. Chest first into the ground. Lunaara Screamed in a flare of raw white light that cracked every cloud above.

Astryn turned his head away glyphs on his shoulder flickering as though unable To hold their shape. Puffin's eyes lost their shine. He stepped forward, no Longer floating, no longer smiling. Nerion was gone and something in the light fractured with him.

The Astryn stood still. Its lights flickered in chaos for the first time they had lost Their shape. The perfect symmetry of its body trembled, and its shoulder crystal Cracked down the side, not from the damage but from grief.

It looked down at Nerion's broken body, cracks appeared on his frosty body. This was a brutal encounter even for Drakaara and Nerion certainly did not Deserve this. This was a major blow to the army of light. And a very shocking One at that.

It shout out a rainbow color light towards the sky making patterns of ancient Ruins that made patterns of an ancient compass. His statement was clear.

"May light be your compass"

An eerie silence had taken over the battlefield. Even Drakaara paused Momentarily with her eyes closed in reverence. Nerion fought well.

Puffin floated forward. No teleportation, no spin, no smile. His lights and Thunders were faded now, His tiny hand began to tremble

He lifted his arms and from his chest burst a ribbon of pure chroma. A spiraling Color beam that twisted like melody through sky. It slammed into Drakaara's Mid section, forcing her back for the first time.

The dark astryn turned.

Its diamond head pulsed with dark energy, its eye slots began to glow. Two rays Of plasma lashed from its face. Puffin flew up dodging the first beam. He Threw a ring of reflective energy below causing deflection. Then came the Second beam, it struck him mid flight and held. The beam did not explode. It Tore.

Puffin's body stretched like steam, his cloudlike form unraveling at the middle And then, It split.

Torn in half like paper. Two sides of joy, drifting apart in silence. His eyes Blinked once from both halves. And then he was gone. A soft drizzle of color Rained down.

The battle paused. The Astryn collapsed to its knees as if praying. Lunaara Lowered her gaze. The battlefield dimmed. The air turned electric but colder Than ice. And for the first time since inception. Kolog's land had lost its music, its trees fallen like Nerion and Puffin. Its pink sky turned grey.

The armies were now equal with Drakaara and Dark Astryn resembling the Army of Darkness whiles Lunaara and the Astryn resembling the army of Light.

Lunaara and the Astryn rose together not flying-Levitating like pulled up by a Divine force. The Astryn's light, its form flickered erratically fueled by Rage. Lunaara's light too flickered, her eyes turned blood red. She wanted revenge. So Together they extended their arms and in the hollow space between their hands. A blinding orb began to form.

It spun slowly at first, gathering their essence, their loss, their fury, their pain, Their rage it glowed in sheer gold. It began to grow slowly from 5 to 15 to 20Feet high. A sphere of pure light.

Across the battlefield Drakaara stepped forward. And beside her, the Dark Astryn raised its hands without command. They too had lost, they too had fury And so with zero ceremony they began to shape their answer.

A sphere emerged slow, suffocating , its edges bleeding black smoke. It dripped The way old nightmares do. Inside the galaxies seemed to fold and die. It began To grow from 5 to 15 to 20 feet high. A sphere of absolute dark. A perfect Answer to the sphere of pure light.

Two spheres both suspended in the heart of war both humming with primordial Power. And then they moved. Not thrown, not fired but drawn towards each Other.

As they neared, the wind fled, the clouds bent into halos and all four. Lunaara, Astryn, Drakaara and Dark Astryn lowered their arms in unison. The orbs Collided.

And "**BANG**" There was an explosion. As huge as the universe. Loud and final. Light tore open, dark unraveled and in that haunted collision

"THE BIG BANG WAS BORN"

The battle field cracked in every direction, Silence spread everywhere like Shroud. The universe trembled. Something new, something scary was Happening. The shockwaves rushed outwards like a cosmic scream. Drakaara Was stunned she had known tremors, she had known shockwaves but this was Different this was not destruction, this was not prison. This was something Opposite. This was creation or at least a form of it. The universe seemed to burn With a smile and from that burn was born

"TIME"

The battle had come to a halt. No one moved. Not because they didn't want to But because they couldn't. They were frozen not in ice, but in awe. For the first Time they witnessed something beyond war, something beyond light and dark.

"The big bang had never happened before"

And in that moment Kolog's skies turned gold for the first time in inception. Above the battlefield, lines of light etch themselves across the sky, weaving in Divine rhythm. They were patterns but not of Lunaara, Drakaara, or the Astryn's these were the patterns of the almighty, of god, Of Eldarion himself. The Gold did not blind, it clarified.

"A thousand symbols spiraled through kolog, their edges, soft their glow Unthreatening. The gold sent to them was reminding them."

Light will never erase the dark, Darkness will never swallow light. Their clash is not the end. But merely the beginning.

THE END

About Author

Mohit Kamlesh Tolani is a passionate writer with a vision to become a globally renowned author. Known for his unique touch in poetry and storytelling, Mohit has made a mark in the literary world by contributing to six acclaimed anthologies: *Zinda Yaden, Shabd Sangini, Safarnama-1, Pride, Ruh-e-Mohabbat, Fakira*,and*Happy New Year*.

His notable achievement includes a nomination in the Guinness Book of World Records for the anthology Ruh-e-Mohabbat, featuring his short poetry titled "The Love Story of Angel and Devil." This poem also inspired his debut theatre play, "Seeds of Desire," showcasing his ability to weave captivating narratives across genres. With his recent feel good short story titled "A light left behind to a mystery thriller titled The Missing Breifcase" published on Ruhemohbbat.

He is now venturing into the journey of becoming an Author with his debut novella Lunaara.

With a deep love for fiction, Mohit continues to craft stories that resonate with readers worldwide. He is committed to creating impactful literary works and aims to establish himself as a celebrated writer on the global stage.

About Publisher

The publisher of this book titled "**Lunnara**" Written by Mohit Kamlesh Tolani is "**Power In Me Foundation.**" As the name suggest it is a Trust that works on sustainable development model. It is established to work for the welfare of the people with rare diseases and their families. Publishing is one of the activities to help raise funds to carry out the activities aimed to creating awareness about various rare diseases, provide scholarships for studies, to provide for livelihood training, to provide for healthcare training, to establish centers for their care and various other objectives for social causes.

The authors associated with us follow the same vision to make the society a better place through their creative writing. We encourage raw talents with time-to-time guidance and exposure through our creative platform Ruh-E-Mohabbat by supporting and promoting them.

For any query on our publishing services, or supporting our cause to create awareness about rare diseases while empowering them you can reach us at mpowerinme@ gmail.com. You can even call/whatsapp at +91-8851537816. Website: www.powerinme.org and www.ruhemohabbat.com

Notes

Notes

Notes